–g: deceleration at units of 32 ft per second^2.

GHA: the Greenwich Hour Angle of a heavenly body measured 0°–360° westward from the Greenwich meridian around the Equator.

gimbals: a mounting for keeping anything in the horizontal or vertical plane regardless of the heel of the ship (compasses, lamps, stoves, etc.).

gnomonic: a chart drawn so that all the meridians of longitude meet at either pole, as on any globe.

GP: the geographical position of any heavenly body, which is the point on the earth's surface directly underneath it. It is a function of declination and Hour Angle.

GPS: Global Position System, a means of giving continuous fixes of high accuracy anywhere in the world. Not yet available to yachtsmen.

Great Circle: the shortest track between any two points on the earth's surface drawn as a straight line on a gnomonic chart, or as a curved one on a Mercator chart, except for courses due N or S.

Greenwich meridian: the N-S line from which all longitude scales are graduated E or W. It happens to pass through the Astronomer Royal's old telescope just up the hill from the National Maritime Museum at Greenwich.

GMT: The time kept between $7\frac{1}{2}°$W and $7\frac{1}{2}°$E without local adjustments such as Summer Time. It is the base for all tables and calculations in celestial navigation.

H$_C$: the tabulated or calculated altitude of any heavenly body at the time of a simultaneous direct observation.

H$_O$: the corrected observed altitude taken at the same time as H$_C$.

HE: the height-of-eye above the water when taking any observation. Its correction was formerly known as Dip.

hockey puck: US slang for a small rubber-framed hand-bearing compass.

hotel load: the electrical power needed to sustain the basic requirements of any boat with electrical instruments and appliances – all the way from navigation lights to deep freezers.

horizontal parallax: an allowance made for the moon because of its relative closeness to offset the fact that its rays do not hit the earth's surface at a single point, but in parallel bands.

hull speed: the theoretical maximum speed of a boat under sail before it planes. It relates to waterline length.

hygrometer: an instrument for reading the specific gravity of the electrolyte in a wet battery. The most accurate measurement of a battery's state of charge.

hyperbolic aids: navigation aids dependent on radio waves emanating from known shore-stations, not dissimilar to the ripples on a pool after a stone has been thrown into it. Decca and Loran-C are examples.

IALA: the International Association of Lighthouse Authorities who seek universal adoption of uniform buoyage and light systems.

impeller: the moving part in a log measuring speed (and distance) by the rotation of a small helical vane let into a protective skeg.

IMS: the International Measurement System, which assesses racing handicaps for boats predominantly intended for cruising.

Inertial Navigation: a means of fixing position by very accurate small gyros and their associated accelerometers measuring the variance from N and S co-ordinates. Not yet available for yachts.

index error: the error in measuring sextant altitudes due to the zero point on the scale being out of alignment.

intercept: the measured distance by which a single position line of a celestial body is from the position arbitrarily assumed for calculating a sight.

IOR: the International Offshore Rule for handicapping yachts. Over the years it has favoured boats with speed but few other attributes.

isobars: lines of equal barometric pressure on a weather map.

isophase: a navigational light which shows its light and eclipse periods at exactly similar intervals.

Jeppesen plotter PJ 1: a light aircraft protractor which is the best for plotting in yachts as well. UK equivalent is Airtour Navigation Plotter (ANZP-1)

kHz: kiloHertz, the measurement of radio frequencies. Formerly known as kilocycles (kc/s).

land breeze: a breeze found in inshore waters after sunset on a long hot day, blowing away from the beach.

LAT: Lowest Astronomical Tide. As the name implies it is the lowest level of water ever to be expected at a given point. For practical purposes it differs little from Low Water Springs.

latitude: lines parallel to the equator marking degrees of arc as projected from the centre of the earth from 0°–90°N or S at the poles. Each degree is 60nm, subdivided by 60 seconds of arc, each

(Continued inside back cover.)

The Shell Guide to Yacht Navigation

by the same author

THE SHELL PILOT TO THE ENGLISH CHANNEL
1. Harbours on the South Coast of England
Ramsgate to the Scillies

THE SHELL PILOT TO THE ENGLISH CHANNEL
2. Harbours in Northern France and the Channel Islands
Dunkerque to Brest

The Shell Guide to Yacht Navigation

Captain J. O. Coote, Royal Navy

A Shell Guide

faber and faber
LONDON · BOSTON

First published in 1987
by Faber and Faber Limited
3 Queen Square London WC1N 3AU

Printed in Great Britain by
Butler & Tanner Ltd., Frome, Somerset

© Captain J. O. Coote, 1987

It is regretted that neither the book's sponsor, nor its author,
nor the publisher can accept responsibility for errors or
omissions, especially those brought about by changes made
by harbour and navigation authorities after the time of
going to press.

The Shell symbol and the name 'Shell' are both trademarks

Although sponsoring this book, Shell UK Ltd would point out
that the author is expressing his own views.

British Library Cataloguing in Publication Data

Coote, J.O.
The Shell guide to yacht navigation.
1. Navigation   2. Yachts and yachting
I. Title
623.89′0247971   VK555

ISBN 0–571–14691–0

For
BENGY
agreeable shipmate,
exciting navigator

CONTENTS

FOREWORD
by Robin Knox-Johnston, C.B.E.

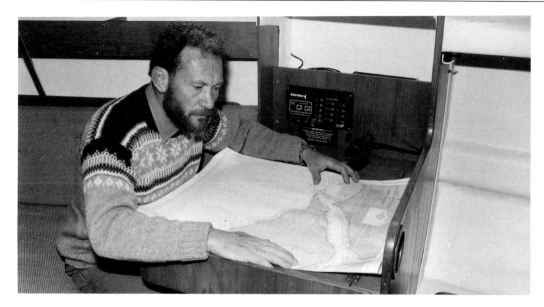

Navigation sounds so simple – just the art of finding your destination from your departure point. It does not matter whether you are going half-way round the world, or just popping along the coast to the next port, you are still going to navigate your way. The differences may seem immense: the one seeing no land for months on end and finding his way by the sun, stars or Sat-Nav; and the other probably doing it all by eye, but both are performing the same function.

The professional navigator learns all sorts of tricks to help him to find his position, and he also learns short cuts to make the job easier. However, he still needs to master the basics, without relying on all the modern aids that have made navigation today so simple. Before the days of Decca, I was a young watchkeeper in a small passenger ship in the Persian Gulf when we ran into a thickish, low-lying sand-storm. Visibility was reduced to a couple of miles, with the horizon obscured from the bridge, when the radar packed up and we were left to find our way by dead reckoning. The Captain decided, however, that he wanted a check. So he had the gangway lowered down to sea-level, and I was sent down with a sextant to get a sight. The trick was to get a clear horizon by reducing the height of eye so that a sight was possible. We got a position-line, made Kuwait in safety, and I had learned another useful lesson.

Modern yacht navigation is increasingly dependent upon electronic aids, which are excellent and very accurate. However, many yachtsmen have not had the time, nor the experience, to learn what to do when the power fails or the fuse blows and these magic aids cease to function. The result can be worry at best, fear at worst, and probably a crew who will be a lot less keen to come sailing again. It is not enough to know how to work the most complicated of modern navigational aids. It is as important to know the basics behind how to navigate, so that, whatever the situation, you have a good idea of where you are and where you should be heading.

These sorts of skill can only be learned from a really experienced navigator, preferably someone who has received a thorough training in the fundamentals, made mistakes over the years and profited from them, and has the ability to pass the knowledge on in an easy-to-understand and amusing manner – as Johnnie Coote demonstrates in this book.

I have always had the greatest respect for those who can navigate completely blind, as a submariner has to beneath the sea, and he learned his trade in submarines. The concentration and sheer professionalism leave their mark. Certainly, years later in 1971, when we sailed together with Sir Max Aitken in *Crusade*, Johnnie was a very wily and accurate navigator. He was also great fun to sail with, and that, fundamentally, is what navigation and sailing should be all about.

AUTHOR'S INTRODUCTION

I address this book to the weekend sailor who wants to graduate from his Wayfarer or Boston whaler in an estuary and go farther afield. It is intended to lift the veil of mystique which surrounds the navigator's art and show that making a coastal or even offshore passage without undue worry or delay is simpler than most cross-country trips on B-roads in the family jalopy.

If he feels like indulging himself in electronic push-button aids to navigation, this book sounds a note of caution on the degree of accuracy and infallibility claimed for most of them.

There are many admirable text-books on the subject, some of them dwelling at greater length than I do on the theory behind the practice. For example, I make no attempt to encourage taking star sights from a yacht, not due to their slightly greater complexity but because the average conditions from the deck of a yacht at twilight are most likely to yield misleading results, even for comparatively experienced navigators.

My approach is to instruct by recalling my own experience of navigating cruising and racing boats in many waters for nearly half a century. There are few mistakes I have not made in my time. It may surprise some that many of the lessons I have learned were drawn from years of blind, three-dimensional navigation in submarines.

The book is enriched by Graham Parrish's meticulous illustrations and by Major-General Jim Gavin's constructive criticism after running his practised eye over my manuscript. Sappers make great navigators, whether finding their way round mine-fields or up Mount Everest.

John Coote
May 1987

Some half-baked people with half-decked dinghies make impressive coastal passages without any aids to navigation beyond a road-map. Ironically they often get away with it. But sooner or later others will have to go out of their way and even risk their necks to get them out of difficulties of their own making.

I am indebted to Captain Ian McKay, the harbour-master at Chichester, for the provenance of the tale of a young couple who sought to oblige a friend by delivering his newly-acquired 21ft dayboat from the Hamble to its new home at Lechlade on the upper reaches of the Thames via the Straits of Dover – a little matter of 300 miles. The voyage ended on the Looe Rocks off Selsey, just 40 miles along the route. When the lifeboat took them off in a rising gale they clutched their sole aid to navigation for the voyage – an AA book. The battered remains of the boat were then lashed on to a borrowed trailer and delivered to the owner via Winchester and Newbury in under four hours.

Neither here nor, surprisingly, in North America is there any statutory inhibition to stop would-be Francis Chichesters from putting down a deposit at the Boat Show and setting sail in a cloud of euphoria. This especially applies to first-time powerboat owners with only a cheque-book or a ferry time-table for a navigation manual.

The easiest way to learn is alongside a practical navigator who has already made most of the classic mistakes and not a few original ones in his time – a fully paid-up member of the Reciprocal Club, or one who failed to note that the chart's depths were in feet and not metres, misidentified a watery light by failing to check its characteristics by stopwatch, or cutting a corner in over-familiar waters on a falling tide without a glance at the chart. As I have done.

He (or she) will soon teach you that the whole art lies in always assuming the worst case until it is proved otherwise. This proposition underlies my efforts to make yacht navigation a matter of common-sense filtering of observed data.

There are other ways to learn. For example some local authorities in the UK and many yacht clubs run winter evening classes based on the syllabuses approved by the Royal Yachting Association (RYA) or the US Coast Guard up to various levels of competence as yacht navigators. You can even get audio or video cassettes to augment the impressive list of text-books on the subject. For details check the classified advertisements in the yachting magazines.

As for our friends who ended up on the rocks off Selsey, I'll send them a copy of this book in the slight hope that they have not lost their taste for seagoing altogether.

For the owner of the average family cruiser who wants to explore not-too-distant horizons there are certain Bare Necessities beyond the inventory of safety equipment needed for sailing in any weather outside the Serpentine (navigation lights, radar reflector, foghorn, safety harnesses and lifejackets). They are:

1 A compass
2 Charts and the means of using them
3 A means of measuring how much water is under the keel
4 A method of measuring distance run and/or speed.

The compass
An accurate compass which can be easily read by the helmsman under all circumstances is essential. It is not an item to economize on. It may end up costing £250 but it will last a

Pedestal steering compass with
rope-guard. B & G instuments set
in athwartships coaming

lifetime. Installing it in the optimum position should take priority over all other considerations.

In a yacht with *wheel steering* the most satisfactory location is on a pedestal in the centre-line immediately before the wheel. Ideally the compass should:

(a) Have a gimballed compass card inside an oil-filled magnified glass bowl with optimum damping against the boat's movement in a sea way. It should be gimballed without interference up to 45° of heel.

(b) Read 0–360° using 1- or 2-figure white numbers in 20° steps. I like to see the cardinal points shown as letters (N, E, S and W), with unnumbered intermediate headings every 5°, but otherwise the card must be simple and easy to read from wherever the helmsman chooses to steer. It is useful if there are gimballed vertical lubber's lines marking the abeam bearings as well as those lined up fore-and-aft. Sitting the boat out to weather, it is easy to sail on a 'minus-90°' course; e.g. while sailing a course of 340°, sit out to starboard and sail the boat on 250° using the port-beam lubber's line. They also permit a crew member to watch the ship's head if the helmsman is concentrating on other instruments.

(c) Have independent illumination of the compass card controlled by an on-off switch and a separate dimmer rheostat located down below under cover. It is undesirable to have the compass illumination on the same switch as the navigation lights.

(d) A detachable non-magnetic binnacle cover is necessary to protect the main compass from damage in harbour. As a rule these fold over to expose the helmsman's side of the compass card, but it is best to stow it below at sea. There is no point in distracting the helmsman by asking for the heading when someone can read off the reciprocal and add 180°.

(e) The means of adjusting the compass (magnets) should be protected against accidental physical interference but easily

For a boat with tiller steering — 2 compasses set in for'ard cockpit bulkhead with instruments overhead

accessible to the adjuster.

For yachts with *tiller steering* there are several options, depending on the size of the cockpit and the likelihood of having other crew-members blocking the helmsman's view of the compass. The criteria outlined above for the pedestal-mounted compass apply wherever practicable.

(f) A bracket-mounted compass being a vertical surface with external gimballing is prone to being snagged by sheets or lurching crew. It can be unshipped and stowed below in harbour, always bearing in mind the risk of upsetting the ship's magnetic error in the compass (deviation).

(g) Shelf-mounted compasses, flush-fitting with the deck or thwart, tend to be sited close to the main magnetic interference (engine, electric cables, magnetic influences in other instruments). On a beamy boat it may be worth having two shelf-mounted compasses, one mounted on deck each side immediately before the helmsman's up-wind steering position. The trouble begins when they disagree with one another.

(h) If the hatchway is in the centre-line, bulkhead-mounted compasses are off-centre. The effect of this is psychological rather than practical. There are also problems lurking the other side of the bulkhead if there are other nav-aids or cables close by. But many such compasses have the bonus of a clinometer measuring the angle of heel under them. This is a much neglected aid to making a boat go faster, if its design is such that it needs to be sailed as nearly upright as possible.

(i) The standard compass can be mounted in the coachroof, subject to the helmsman's clear view of it in all conditions.

(j) A recent development is to depend on remote-reading displays transmitted from a master compass. One such system – as it happens one of the best – which co-ordinates all nav-aids into a comprehensive system of compatible displays (Travacrest) has even abandoned the use of the word compass by calling it the 'Heading Reference Unit'. Once you accustom yourself to a digital display of the ship's heading it has some advantages: for a start the numbers are big enough to read, even by a helmsman with spray-drenched spectacles. Once the master compass has been tucked away far from all local interference it has a high degree of built-in stability. There is no reason why it should lose anything in transmitting to a slave display unit.

Compasses for *powerboats* need not cater for more than 15° angle of heel but should have shock-proof mounting and be sufficiently damped to keep a steady ship's head. Many have an external 0–360° ring which can be slewed round to get the desired course on to the lubber line. The helmsman then has to keep to the ordered course by aligning the compass card to the external ring.

Generally the steering compass in a powerboat is well away from the main source of the ship's magnetic interference – the engine. It is desirable to have it mounted so that it lies on or near the helmsman's line-of-sight while looking ahead. The quality of lookout which a helmsman can maintain within a sheltered wheel-house is in any event greatly inferior to that from an open position, so the less distraction he has the better. That is why I prefer a compass suspended from overhead (see p. 41).

Secondary Compass
Although modern steering compasses are reliable and surprisingly accurate within their known limits of error (see p. 21) it is essential to have a spare primary compass on board. In a small boat a *hand-bearing compass* can serve this purpose.

Ex-Navy handbearing compass

Batteries

These come in many shapes and sizes, dating back to the cumbersome ex-Service teak-handled bowl variety with optical bearing prism. The handle's size was determined by the batteries needed to provide illumination, but nowadays most have built-in fluorescent lighting. These need a secure, dry stowage of their own, so are not as readily available on deck as they should be when the need arises. They weigh 3lb each.

Far the best type is the 3in-diameter mini-compass held in a 1in-deep rubber collar. In the States it is referred to as the 'hockey puck'. A tritium gas capsule (or Beta Light) provides excellent lighting. The human hand is as good as most gyro-stabilized gimbals, so excellent bearings can be obtained, provided always that you give them time to settle down after being yanked out of your oilskin pocket or wherever else it is

Stowage

Rubber covered handbearing compass with Beta-light

stowed. In a jump of sea, when the compass card swings over and above the helmsman chasing the lubber line, it is essential to wait for a mean reading at either end of the swing.

Hand-bearing compasses have eliminated the need for azimuth rings or any other means of taking bearings directly from the steering compass by standing abaft the helmsman and observing the compass heading off the ship's fore-and-aft line.

A fair calibrating point for the latter is to put a bit of boat-tape on the after end of the superstructure in transit with the base of the mast, having first verified it from the lubber line on the steering compass.

The hand-bearing compass is essential for watching the bearing of a converging ship or of progress against the tide on a passing headland – or a competing boat in a race. It is also the best way of checking the steering compass on an ocean passage using the azimuth of the sun when it is very low on the horizon (see p. 21). There are binoculars on sale with a bearing compass built-in, but their field of view is too restricted, especially in a jump of sea.

Except in an emergency it is not practical to use the hand-bearing compass as a substitute steering compass. A small bracket-mounted compass (only 5in in diameter) in the vicinity of the chart-table not only gives the navigator an on-the-spot check on the course being steered, but can be pressed into service as an alternate steering compass (see p. 46). This does not rate as one of the Bare Necessities, but at around £50 it costs little more than the hand-bearing compass.

Finally if you have a radio D/F set it will have a small compass as part of the hand-held antenna, but I would not rate this as better than ± 10° accuracy, no matter what the makers claim.

Installation

Most stock boats are sold with the compass already installed as the only standard nav-aid. The rest, from echo-sounder to wind indicators, are customer options. Even so it is as well to check that the compass is fitted to the requirements listed above and is not affected by the motor or any electronic devices running. It is a fundamental requirement that the lubber line is set fore-and-aft. This is a matter best left to a boatyard.

Compass Errors

There are two variable sources of compass error which distinguish a magnetic compass from a gyro-compass reading degrees True. That is, on the normal mercator's-projection charts which we use, True North (360°T) is the vertical axis of the chart, up and down the page.

But magnetic compasses seek the North magnetic pole, which is a slowly meandering point located in the Arctic wastes nor'west of Greenland. This is 360°M. The first correction to be applied between the two is known as *Variation*. It is shown on the compass rose of all Admiralty charts as a separate pointer towards North (magnetic) which slews all the other 360° magnetic headings with it.

Thus a current English Channel chart will show the variation to be anywhere between 5°W and 10°W, depending on how far west you are. Alongside the legend on the compass rose is the year on which this was correct, with a small annual correction to allow for the magnetic North Pole's meandering around. Take a typical chart in the western end of the Channel. The variation is shown as 8°28′West in 1981, decreasing by 8 minutes annually. In 1986 the variation therefore becomes 8°28′W minus 40 minutes (5 × 8), making 7°48′W. Unless you are using a very old chart, the difference is minimal and can be ignored.

The other correction is to take account of the errors induced by local magnetic fields in the boat and its equipment. This is known as *Deviation* and has to be added or subtracted to the variation.

Think True

Make a determined effort to get into the habit of navigating at all times in degrees True, because those are the lines you are going to draw on the chart. Furthermore all the information given on charts or in other navigation publications are in degrees True.

There are various mental aids to translate magnetic to True, of which the best known is:

Variation West – Compass best (higher number of degrees)
Variation East – Compass least (lower number of degrees)

This means simply that 10°W variation will have the effect of the ship's magnetic compass reading 10° higher than True. Thus 250°M is the same as 240°T. If in doubt, as one sometimes is when tired or sailing in unaccustomed parts of the world, line up your parallel ruler on the compass rose to read 250°M and you will see on the outer ring that it is 240°T.

Exactly the same applies with Deviation. The slight complication is that a Deviation with a contrary name to the Variation has to be applied accordingly:

Variation 10°W   Deviation3°W means that 240°T is the same as 253°M. Whereas
Variation 10°W   Deviation 3°E   results in 240°T being 247°M.

Always remember that while the navigation and general picture is being conducted in degrees True, the helmsman and any information from bearings observed will be in degrees magnetic. Don't attempt to confuse that issue, until the day when we have gyro-compasses in yachts. The helmsman's ordered course must be always magnetic.

Compass Corrections and Adjustment

On first installation the steering compass should be checked and adjusted professionally. Any marina office will produce an expert who will take the boat out with you and do this. First there will be a 360° swing through the cardinal points to identify the compass error on each 45° heading (deviation). By moving magnets close to the compass card, these errors can be reduced or eliminated.

At the end of the day you will be presented with a Deviation Card and Certificate of Correction which should reduce Deviation to less than 3° on any heading. Usually it comes down to a figure so small that it can be ignored, except on long passages. The errors shown on the card should be symmetrical about Nil error (i.e. maximum W'ly deviation should be nearly, but not exactly matched by the highest E'ly deviation).

Deviation Card

STEERING COMPASS

Yacht: *Lulubelle XIII*

Date: 13 May 1987

Magnetic Course	Deviation	Compass Course
000°	1°E	359°
015°	1°E	014°
030°	2°E	028°
045°	3°E	042°
060°	3°E	057°
075°	2°E	073°
090°	1°E	089°
105°	1°E	104°
130°	0	130°
145°	0	145°
165°	1°W	166°
180°	1°W	181°
↓		
360°		

Signed: J. M. Fingers

To steer a given magnetic course, the actual compass course to be steered is shown in the right column.

Don't forget this applies only to the steering compass, so others, like the hand-bearing compass, do not have this fine tuning. Nor do they need it, since the accuracy of bearings read from them is usually well outside the swing of Deviations; in any case it will vary with the proximity of major ship's sources of magnetic interference on each occasion of taking a bearing.

There is much advice on how frequently the compass should be professionally checked and adjusted. The fact is that it need not be done unless it is seen to be necessary as the result of your own *ad hoc* checks. These are most important and should be carried out whenever the boat has been laid up ashore or left lying alongside on a constant heading for any length of time. It is dead simple. Take any distant transit of charted conspicuous points ashore and read off the compass heading when it is lined up ahead. Repeat the process with the transit dead astern. But if time does not permit, at least take a reading going along well-marked fairways, such as down the Hamble River, where the true course can be taken off the chart.

On an ocean passage the best check on your compass is to take an azimuth (bearing) of any celestial body, but preferably the sun at low altitude. This is especially necessary in a steel boat. The easiest way is to take the sun's bearing when its lower limb is within half its diameter of the observed horizon. First you should know your latitude and declination to within 1°. Then simply enter the tables in *Reed's* Section V 'Sun's True Bearing at Sunrise or Sunset' or *Macmillan's Almanac* Ch. 3, Tab. 3(1). You can work it out ahead of time.

Thus for latitude 51°N and declination 10°N the sun's bearing on rising will be 074°True (N74°E). If the declination is 10°S then the True bearing would be 74° anticlockwise from due south or S74°E (i.e. 180° − 74° = 106°True).

Apply Variation to determine the compass error. The deviation will only be correct for the ship's heading at the time of observation.

The easiest way is to point the boat directly at or away from the sun at the moment. Or use a hand-bearing compass.

Modern yacht compasses are reliable and surprisingly accurate, so don't worry unduly that they may suddenly let you down. Just watch out for the introduction of a new source of magnetic interference. I know of a steering compass which was mysteriously thrown off when a jerrican was moved from one end of the cockpit locker to the other.

Once there was a cadet at Dartmouth who was so unhappy that he decided to 'borrow' a 45ft Admiralty launch and head for Spain. He did all his chartwork before creeping away during the middle watch, setting a course from Start Point to Ushant. Dawn found him off Alderney, where he was apprehended. He had no reason to believe that the compass had not been swung or adjusted for years. Yet when the police boarded him he declined a cigarette because smoking was forbidden at the College. His log showed that he had carefully switched off the motor for five minutes each hour, as he had been taught.

Charts

No matter what size or type of boat you sail in, if you intend taking it outside your local harbour limits a suitable inventory of up-to-date charts is essential.

It used to be the practice of chart agents to date-stamp each chart on the day you bought it. I make a point of noting it alongside the title in pencil. Next look to see when the chart was printed and the number of the latest small correction made as a result of a Notice to Mariners. On Admiralty charts all this information is on the bottom of the chart.

Imray charts give the date of printing inside the first cover and have a resumé of recent corrections on a fly-sheet.

In 1950 I joined *Fandango* for the Santander Race returning via a race to Belle Île and cruising home. The owner was Gerald Potter, an unforgettable hairshirt Grenadier-turned-fisherman. I looked over the charts and found that they had all been bought from J. D. Potter in June 1934. The suggestion that 16 years and a World War might have outdated some of the musty old charts was brushed aside. 'I believe that the rocks don't move, so what's the matter with you?'

As the price of charts rockets ever upwards – twentyfold since the 'fifties – the temptation to go on using old charts must be strong. In theory there is no reason why they should not be maintained up to date by small ink corrections, but they may sooner or later be over-cluttered. Nevertheless at £6.90 each (1987) for a standard Admiralty chart, one can sympathize with those who carry a few charts stamped 'Not to be used for navigation'.

When asking for one, always check the catalogued number of the chart, or you may end up with one that is useless for your voyage. On the 1960 Transatlantic Race we didn't plan a stop in Newfoundland, so carried no local charts of that area. A week out of Bermuda we found ourselves heading for St John's under jury rig. After hailing a German freighter we ended up doing a heaving-line transfer of a bottle of Scotch one way in return for a rolled-up chart. It was not until she was beyond recall that I found we had acquired an up-to-date chart of St John, New Brunswick.

In case you think that was stupid, there is also a St John's in Antigua, and others in the Red Sea and Florida, while St John can be found in the Virgin Islands, Liberia and sou'west of Hong Kong. But I did wonder if that kraut knocking off our bottle of Black Label gave a moment's thought to how we were going to make a thousand miles to windward against the Gulf Stream without a mast.

If you want to cruise to North Brittany and carry all the Admiralty charts and publications you need, allowing for unscheduled stops due to weather, there will be little change out of £250, including tidal atlases and relevant pilotage books. Or, a navigator may spend £350 before a Fastnet Race, including harbour plans for every funkhole around the track. Some yacht clubs have negotiated discounts for their members which should be pursued.

Recognizing this, the private chart publishers on both sides of the Channel (Imray, Stanford and Carte-Guide) publish general charts with a substantial number of inset large-scale harbour plans. Thus Imray's North Foreland to Beachy Head chart (C.8) has seven such plans for harbours all for £5.95. To cover the same harbours by buying separate Admiralty charts would cost over £40, albeit projecting each harbour on a bigger scale. The Imray inset harbour plans are perfectly adequate for taking a yacht in and out of harbour, but are mostly too small to lay off fixes.

The other sources of harbour plans are pilotage books. Although these mostly incorporate stern legal waivers about not being suitable for navigation except as complementary to established charts, they should not be overlooked, if only for the amount of information they give for around £15. The charts in them may be over-simplified or no more than a thumbnail sketch of the port layout, but some (such as in the *Shell Pilot to the English Channel*) are a lot better than none. Some, like Robin Brandon's *Pilots*, published by Imray, and Malcolm Robson's *French Pilots* (Nautical Publishing) go into immense detail, especially for those interested in rock-hopping to find quiet, barely frequented anchorages, are more suitable than any recognized charts.

Sailing a 32ft Beneteau from Cork to Hamble in March we ran into persistent strong easterlies off the Lizard and made little progress even with the motor running. Soon it was

evident that we should need to put into Falmouth for fuel. Our only chart was from the Lizard to Start Point on a scale 2 miles to the inch which made Falmouth look small. The scale in the *Shell Pilot* was nearly $2\frac{1}{2}$ times larger, so we had no problem using it all the way to the fuel dock at the Marina.

There will always be times when one has to make do with other than the charts or publications approved by RYA yachtmaster examiners. Bringing *Roundabout* back from Copenhagen after the 1966 World One-Ton Cup we had no intention of going through the Dutch canals, because we had only 8 days to be back for Cowes Week. Somewhere off Borkum we were laying a course for Whitby on port tack in a full W'ly gale, making painfully slow and uncomfortable progress.

There was a brief crew meeting before we were off broad-reaching for the mouth of the Ems. We had a general chart covering Helgoland to the Friesian Islands on a scale of 2 miles to the inch, but it ran out of ideas just short of Delfzijl which we knew to be port of entry to the canal linking the Ems with Zuider Zee – or Haslemere, as we soon learnt to call it (Ijsselmeer). All we could get there was a Shell road map of the Netherlands. It was sufficient to get us first to Groningen for an overnight stop and then on the Lemmer at the north-eastern corner of the Ijsselmeer. Everytime we met a trading barge we had to haul into the bank, which usually meant grounding in soft mud. Back in Cowes no one could figure why the spinnaker pole fittings were clogged with mud. They had been used repeatedly for punting us back into the channel.

We stopped in Lemmer long enough to watch England beat Portugal in the semi-final of the World Cup, then beat against a stiff sou'wester across the Ijsselmeer using a general chart of the southern North Sea. From Amsterdam down to Ijmuiden our road map did us proud. The ensuing gear-busting dead beat to windward in a succession of gales was navigated with a proper outfit of Admiralty charts and publications.

Prices of foreign charts bought in their country of origin are always significantly lower, a point to be borne in mind when ordering up for a cruise.

Chart Scales

The natural scale of charts is always printed under its title on the chart itself or alongside its reference number in the catalogue. This refers to the scale at mid-latitude on the area covered by the chart expressed as a ratio (e.g. 1:125,000).

To avoid buying more charts than you need, it is as well to have an idea of what these ratios mean expressed as miles or yards to the inch on the chart. The following scale is approximate, but will help to put the chart in perspective before ordering it.

Natural Scale	Miles/yards per inch
1:5,000	140yds to 1in (0.07nm)
1:10,000	275yds to 1in (0.14nm)
1:15,000	400yds to 1in (0.2nm)
1:20,000	550yds to 1in (0.275nm)
1:50,000	1,350yds to 1in (0.68nm)
1:75,000	1nm to 1in
1:100,000	1.4nm to 1in
1:150,000	2nm to 1in
1:300,000	4nm to 1in
1:500,000	6.7nm to 1in

Harbour plans or charts

These should ideally be 1:20,000 or larger scale which means lower numbers (see table above). For example, the Admiralty charts for Chichester Harbour (3418) and that for Weymouth and Portland (2255) are both 1:20,000. This is not a hard and fast rule, especially for deepwater ports. There is no point in buying the 1:10,000 large-scale chart of Cherbourg Harbour (2602) when the 1:50,000 scale of C. de la Hague to Barfleur (1106) shows Cherbourg Harbour at 0.68nm to one inch.

Coastal Charts

It is helpful to plot a passage on a succession of charts of the same scale. You cover from Beachy Head to the Lizard with three adjoining Admiralty charts (2450, 2454, and 442). These are all at a suitably accurate scale for plotting by fixes or dead reckoning 1:150,000, which is 2nm to the inch. The famous Channel Islands and Adjacent Coasts of France chart (2669) is the same scale.

Planning Charts

These are small scale, useful for laying off courses and distances for most of one's voyage. For example, one Admiralty chart (2675) covers the English Channel from the Scillies to the Dover Straits at a scale of 1:500,000, which is 6.7nm to the inch.

Or you can have one covering the whole of the British Isles (2) on a scale of 1:1,500,000, approximately 20nm to the inch.

Which Charts?

Assuming equality of coverage and data presentation choose the charts you are accustomed to or feel comfortable with.

Admiralty Charts

The Hydrographer of the Navy and his predecessors have

been at the surveying and cartography business since Captain Cook's days, longer than anyone else still in business, and should be the best. Their standard charts are delivered folded (usually only once) to 21in × 28in, opening out to 42in × 28in across. They are printed on heavy stock which survives dripping oilskins or most slopped drinks, but are soon reduced to a soggy mess if left on deck in bad weather. I always carry a zip-up clear plastic envelope big enough to accommodate an open folded chart for use on deck, for example in negotiating a long stretch of eyeball pilotage in wet weather.

They are printed with all symbols and notations in black except for small violet teardrops marking lights on buoys, or solid structures. Coloured areas fall within the following conventions:

Ochre — land exposed at all times

Olive Green — foreshore, banks or rocks which dry out when the tide recedes to chart datum (usually to LAT — lowest astronomical tide — not too different from Low Water Springs)

Sky Blue — depths of 5metres (16½ft) or less at any tide. The next contour 10metres (33ft) may be outlined by a narrow blue tint showing the precise edge of the contour.

White — water with a least depth of over 5metres. In some cases the dividing line between blue and white may be drawn at different depths to the example just given. But a glance at the depths either side of each contour will clarify that point.

No matter how experienced you may be, always have the Admiralty publication 5011 – *Symbols and Abbreviations used in Admiralty Charts* – near at hand. It is invaluable if you find yourself with a few old fathoms-and-feet charts (pre-1985) in which many of the symbols are different.

The scope of chart symbols gradually being introduced includes guidance telling visiting yachtsmen where their most common needs may be found within walking distance of landing points. The most important of these are (always shown violet or white-on-violet):

⚓	Visitors' mooring	⚑	Yacht Club
Ⓥ	Visitors' Berths	🛢	Fuel
▬	Slipway	☎	Pay phone
⊐	Pub	🅟	Parking
⚓	Water supply	⊠	Post office
⚓	Harbour Master's Office	⊖	Customs
Ⓐ	Marina	WC	Public toilets
⚓	Public Landing	⊙	Launderette

The worldwide catalogue of Admiralty charts and publications (NP131) is too expensive (£10) and cumbersome to be carried in most boats, even if it was necessary. It can always be found in any chandlery or authorized chart agent, but need only be consulted if going foreign.

A small folded *Home Waters Catalogue* (NP109) can be obtained free of charge from the same source. It covers from the Arctic Circle to the Gironde, the North Sea and Skaggerak to 10°E and out to 15°W in the Western Approaches. Note, it does not cover the Baltic or Oslo Fjord. It is perfectly adequate for planning most cruises around NW Europe, excepting that the charts are listed only by their numbers, not by their title: e.g. Owers to Beachy Head is shown as a rectangular block on the South Coast, but identified only as 'Chart 1652', last published in 1982, has a Decca lattice chart available and is on scale 1:75,000 (1 mile to the inch).

Corrections to Admiralty Charts

Corrections needed to the whole range of Admiralty charts and publications are promulgated by weekly Notices to Mariners, available free from any agent. Urgent temporary notices may be broadcast by VHF shore radio stations, generally before their local weather forecast.

For yachtsmen there is a special *Small Craft Edition* (NP246) published in February, May, July and September. This confines itself to changes in waters where the depth is less than 23ft (7 metres) and thus relevant to yacht navigation. The area covered is NW Europe. For those sailing in these waters these corrections are perfectly adequate, always bearing in mind that there is a variable time delay of up to 6 months between a change being reported to the Hydrographer and its being promulgated.

The *Small Craft Edition of N to M* also lists all Admiralty chart agents, the next quarter's times of HW and LW Dover and all the principal ports in the area.

Imray Yachting Charts

These are all coloured charts, generally sold in a concertina fold (like a road map) at a standard size $10\frac{1}{4}$in × $5\frac{1}{2}$in when folded. They can also be bought unfolded (31in × 44in) which is 3in bigger than the standard Admiralty chart.

The most versatile range is their C Series which cover the whole English Channel, the East Coast as far as Newcastle and the West Coast as far as Oban, but excluding the Atlantic Coast from Dingle Bay to Donegal. All the charts carry a number of harbour plans as insets. They are cheaper than the Admiralty charts, but suffer from the minor irritation when transferring from one chart to the next that adjacent charts are not always on the same scale.

There is also the 'Y' series, small format for boats with limited chart table space. These are mostly unfolded at $17\frac{1}{2}$in × $25\frac{1}{2}$in but only cover inshore, estuary and harbour charts on the coast of England between Falmouth and the Wash, with one of the Isle of Man as well. They are mostly £3.95 each.

At the time of purchase, each Imray chart shows its date of issue with all the outstanding corrections needed to be made on a correction slip pasted inside the back fold. Up-dated correction slips can be obtained from their stockists at 20p each. Or for £2 p.a. you can get *Norrie's Bulletin of Corrections*, usually six issues a year.

Stanford Charts (Published by Barnacle Marine)

These cover the English Channel, Bristol Channel and southern North Sea in a set of 19 small-scale charts with many large-scale harbour plans.

A list of outstanding corrections will be supplied on receipt of a stamped addressed envelope. The printing date of the chart should be quoted.

French Navy Charts

These are usually single-fold 21in × $29\frac{1}{2}$in, thus being wider than Admiralty charts. All their modern charts are coloured, following a similar pattern to those on Admiralty charts except that the land is shown in beige, the foreshore in grey and most shades of blue to delineate shallow waters: the darker cover depths out to 5m and then a lighter shade out to the 10m contour.

Other points which need familiarization are:
They have no compass rose, but show a small red arrow indicating local Variation canted off a N–S longitude coordinate.

The abbreviations against light characteristics can be confusing.

Q = Quick Flashing becomes 'Scint' or 'Sc' on French charts.

Fl = Flashing is shown as 'é'.

G = Green is 'V' (vert).

Part 2 of the *Shell Pilot for the English Channel* carries a useful glossary. The Admiralty List of Lights (NP74) has a comprehensive one.

Older French charts (pre-colour) have all their vital information in minuscule print.

The French chart service is called SHOM (Service Hydrographique et Océanographique de la Marine). They issue a free brochure catalogue similar to the *Admiralty Home Waters Catalogue*, covering the coasts of France and neighbouring countries – from Dunkerque to the Western Mediterranean as far as Sicily. They are of interest to foreign yachtsmen mostly for providing charts in a few places where other detailed ones do not exist or are on an unsuitable scale (e.g. the Rance from St Malo southwards).

Carte-Guide Coastal Navigation Charts

These are full-colour charts 6½in × 12in (when folded) covering the whole coast of France with overlapping 1:50,000 charts and larger scale harbour plans where necessary. Thus to cover Dieppe to the Alderney Race you need four charts. At this scale you need a more general chart on which to lay off and plot a course between distant points. They are printed on medium-weight paper which is billed as water-resistant.

Their catalogue is shown on the front cover, as the Michelin road maps do.

They have their own symbols and technicolour presentation, but it is all carefully explained on each chart in French and one of 4 other European languages. So spend some time getting the hang of the layout and symbols, for these are outstandingly useful charts, although somewhat daunting in their proliferation of detail.

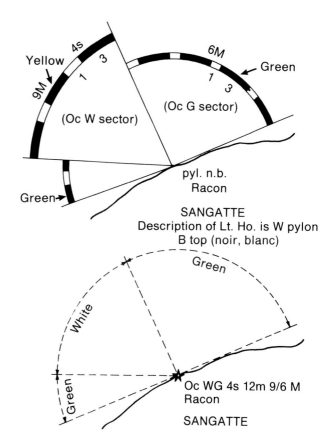

SANGATTE
Description of Lt. Ho. is W pylon
B top (noir, blanc)

Oc WG 4s 12m 9/6 M
Racon

SANGATTE

Same lighthouse as shown on Carte Guide (top) and Imray Charts (below)

Each light shows its characteristics schematically on a radius drawn at its notional limits of visibility. The colour of the light is shown yellow for a white light, otherwise they are self-evident. The eclipse (i.e. dark) period is left blank. The timing of each cycle is shown in minuscule figures around the radius of the light's visibility giving the precise timing of the flashes (see p. 27).

There is a 360°True and magnetic compass rose, and close inshore tidal current arrows and a fascinating compass presentation of the incidence, direction and strengths of the observed winds during April to September.

Carte Guide System
for Fl G 4s with
4M range. G 'spokes'
show 1 sec G flash after
3 secs eclipse

Same buoy
as shown
on Imray
Chart

All the buoys and beacons are shown large enough to save having to turn to the IALA system diagram to identify them. A whistle buoy is marked 'SS' on French charts.

The land is shown pale yellow with all the roads correctly designated by number (N130, D524, etc.). These charts score over others by the extent of the information they give about what can be seen inland from seaward.

Drying-out foreshore is shown in bright yellow for sand or as rose clusters for rocks. The blue tint goes out to the 3metres depth contour.

The scale of their harbour plans tends to be too small for comfort.

These charts are available in any Librairie Maritime. A stamped addressed envelope to their publishers will get the corrections. Mercifully corrections to French charts are needed much less frequently than those covering UK waters.

US and Canadian Charts

These are flat, unfolded at 46in × 30in size, issued by the National Oceanographic and Atmospheric Administration (NOAA) and the Hydrographic Chart Distribution Office: Department of Energy, Mines and Resources, Ottawa, Canada. Excellent in many ways, but you only get all the buoys and beacons on the largest scale charts; so you can be caught short for lack of detailed information, as I was approaching the Bras d'Or Lakes in fog. It is painfully recalled later in this book.

Most yachtsmen on the US Atlantic coast use BBA Chart Kits, which are 9 volumes of US Government Charts reproduced in 22in × 17in format, covering from Nova Scotia to the Virgin Islands. Each has Loran-C grids and consists of a medium-scale chart covering about 100 miles of coastline, followed by a succession of larger-scale local charts, with aerial colour pictures. The kits are not ideal for covering a long cruise, since you find yourself having to move from one chart to another many pages farther on. But they are good for coastal racing or cruising. Their great virtue is the 85% saving they represent against buying a full set of originals.

Gnomonic charts

These are constructed with all the meridians of longitude

meeting at the Poles. They are commonly found in atlases depicting Antarctica or the seas north of Spitzbergen and the Bering Strait. Their practical use for yacht navigators is to determine the Great Circle (GC) course and distance on a long passage in comparatively high latitudes. If you are planning a GC route from Bermuda to the Scillies, lay off a straight line on the gnomonic chart from St David's Head to the Bishop Rock and take a succession of course readings as the line crosses the meridians 10° apart. You will set sail on 050° and make your landfall 2,760 miles later steering 088°.

Mercatorial Plots

All charts in normal use are constructed on Mercator's projection wherein the longitudes are always at right angles to the parallels of latitude. The price to be paid for this convenience is that the latitude scale at either side of the chart is the only one giving the correct distances. For ocean passages it is desirable to have mercatorial plotting sheets in which the latitudes are numbered, but the degrees of longitude can be marked by the navigator to cover wherever he happens to be sailing. They are obtainable on both sides of the Atlantic covering up to 10° of lat and long. But it is easy enough to construct your own, either by using a calculator to solve the equation that 1° of latitude is drawn on a plot for, say, 45°N or S as secant 45°. Or it can be constructed by marking off your desired longitude scale, drawing a line at 45° to it from one end, then ruling off a series of perpendicular lines. Where they cut the oblique 45° line you can measure the latitude scale along that line (see diagram on right).

Oceanic Plotting Sheets are available on a scale of 1:250,000 (3.4nm to the inch) in 6° bands of latitude. Thus 48°–54° is Admiralty Chart 5437. There are corresponding US mercatorial plotting sheets. Sheets for plotting at a much greater scale, complete with their own compass rose, are obtainable

To construct a Mercatorial Plotting Sheet using any convenient longitude scale

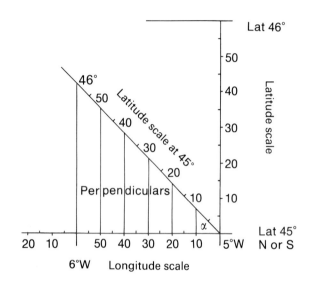

α = angle in degrees from horizontal corresponding to latitude

for plotting out celestial observations.

A mercatorial plot is essential if you find that the ordinary charts for your track are on too small a scale and will not permit accurate EP plotting. This is the case on the Bermuda Race.

Dover Tide Ready Reckoner

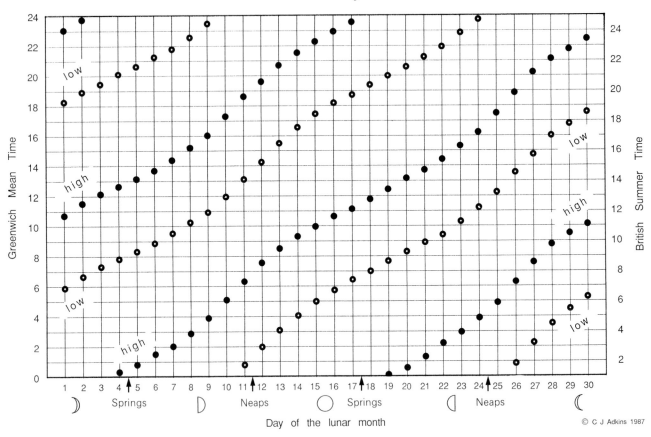

© C J Adkins 1987

Manuals and publications

If you are not planning to go far afield, all you need to supplement the information on your charts are local tide tables. These are often provided free at chandleries or marina offices, but the *Yachting World* diary tells you most of what you need to know by reference to the times of HW and LW at Dover. It also carries tidal atlases for the British Isles and the Solent. There are many pilotage books, tidal atlases and almanacs giving much fuller information (notably the *Shell Pilots* covering the Channel, which are companion volumes to this one).

Failing that, if you remember that the highest tides (Springs) at greatest range occur at Dover around mid-day and midnight, 2–3 days after a full or new moon. The smallest ones (Neaps) occur a week either side of Springs soon after the first and last quarters of the moon. As a rough guide the time of HW is 40 minutes later each day: thus three days after Springs it will be two hours later, and so on. See Adkins Dover Tide Ready Reckoner (opposite)

The farther west you go in the Channel, the earlier the times of HW and LW become relevant to Dover. As far as Portsmouth, time differences are negligible – under half an hour either way. Cherbourg is about 3 hours earlier, the Channel Islands and Weymouth $4\frac{1}{2}$ hours and Cornwall 6 hours before Dover. These are only approximations to be resorted to in case you left the tide tables in your office. Allow for French time being 1 hour ahead, otherwise all these times are GMT, so add one hour during Summer Time. But watch out in the Solent, where there are unsuspected traps like double high waters and long stands.

Plotting and other basic nav-aids

Pencil (B or 2B) with rubber on one end.
Eraser soft white rubber.

Chart table rack for pencils, dividers, compass rubber

Dividers preferably robust brass ones with steel tips, about 6–8in long, preferably those that can be opened and closed with one hand. These should be stowed vertically, near at hand to the chart working surface. Spares for all of them should be in a separate drawer, together with a pencil sharpener (maxi-yachts go for electrically operated pencil sharpeners, but you might go so far as to have the type which collects its own shavings in a screw-on cartridge). In the same drawer should be the navigator's pencil, torch and spare spectacles – or a magnifying glass. Also lens papers for cleaning binoculars.

Magnifying glass with light

Lattice parallel ruler (seldom room for operation)

Parallel rulers (unstable in a yacht)

Parallel ruler or protractor There is a wide variety available. The most unsuitable for yachts are the traditional ones: either those which have their own rollers built-in or those which open and shut on swinging lattice arms which enable you to transfer a bearing from a compass rose to the required point on the chart, or vice versa, by a maddening crab-walk. Those heavy old brass roller parallel rulers are dangerous in a small boat. They are liable to slip while being used, or run out of chart surface to move on.

There are several satisfactory protractors which have a rotating arm about the centre of a square grid, any of

Protractors aligned to lat. or long. lines as datum

Set-square with angles 0-180°

0·360° protractor for use by alignment to lat. or long.

Hurst plotter

32

whose verticals can be aligned to a meridian or horizontals to an E–W latitude co-ordinate. You set the centre of the protractor over the point from which a bearing is to be laid off and swing the arm to the 0–360° reading desired. The line can then be drawn on the straight edge of the plotting arm. Some of these also can have the Variation screwed in as a fixed correction. Of these the Hurst Protractor may be the most popular (see p. 32).

Some navigators use right-angle set-squares, sliding them along a straight surface, but they also depend on nothing slipping during the chartwork.

In the early 'sixties I was taking part in the Miami-Nassau powerboat race, when I met the winner of the Powderpuff Derby (Grannies racing light aircraft across the States). She introduced me to the Jeppesen plotter PJ1 which is so far superior to any other yacht protractor that I never travel without one. It is only 13in × 5½in, is easily stowed, simple to

Jeppesen Plotter and dividers

Aligned with latitude

Read off bearing

line up to any bearing (magnetic or True) and retains its alignment to any co-ordinate by friction alone. So it is ideal for transferring courses or bearings from one chart to another. More importantly, it is the fastest plotter afloat.

The standard article is marketed from Englewood, Colorado, has a scale of statute miles to light aircraft requirements (1:1,500,000), but I have superimposed a scale 1:150,000 at mid-latitude 50° for UK use. Obtainable from suppliers of air navigation maps and instruments. The UK equivalent is the Airtour Navigation Plotter (ANZP1).

Clocks

A ship's clock is also a necessity. Nowadays most sailors have quartz wristwatches, some with digital read-out in hours, minutes and seconds, although they seem to be going out of fashion. I have a 1960 waterproof analogue Ingersoll with a re-setting stopwatch which is also invaluable in, for example, timing light characteristics. I keep an old Rolex Oyster set on GMT as a spare. The old days of a gimballed chronometer in a brass-bound mahogany case, with the deck watch error (DWE) recorded daily, are gone for ever.

They have left me with one abiding memory – losing the 1969 Fastnet in *Crusade* by 68 seconds on corrected time after unsuccessfully protesting the Race Committee for taking the elapsed time five minutes in error. We recorded the finishing time on board from our chronometer a few minutes after it had been checked against the BBC pips for 0900. All the finishing times were noted by a dockyard employee in the Breakwater Fort from a wall-clock with an unsynchronized sweep second hand. Watching from the lawn of Admiralty House was the Flag Officer himself, already late for 0900 meeting. As soon as he saw our saffron spinnaker drop, he noted the time on his wrist-watch, for which he later showed the jury that he had kept its daily error from the 0800 time-signal every day for the last three months.

Nevertheless the protest was thrown out, which was hardly surprising. The night before the Protest Committee convened, one of the hierarchy of the RORC chanced to meet the Flag Officer Plymouth, without realizing who he was since he was in plain clothes. The Admiral was assured that *Crusade* would not be allowed to win the Fastnet on a protest, no matter how strong the evidence in her favour.

The winner had not been reported round the Bishop Rock 98 miles away when we secured alongside Mount Wise, so had to average better than 7kts to win. She did.

It happened to be my birthday. The Admiral's present to me was the current synoptic weather chart. Between Plymouth and the Lizard there was a beautiful col – a zone of no pressure differential with theoretically no wind at all.

Later it was found that both boats had raced under incorrect ratings, to the extent that the finishing time could have been recorded over an hour wrong without depriving us of the Fastnet. But that is another story.

Binoculars

These, as an aid to the legendary MkI Eyeball, are also on the must list. There is no sensible choice other than rubber-bonded 7 × 50s with individual eyepiece focusing. The 7 describes the power magnification: the 50 is the field of view in mm. Chandleries will offer 8 × 30 or even 10 × 70, but the pedigree of the 7 × 50 is unanswerable. In World War II most of the navies of the world started with different sized binoculars, but all ended with 7 × 50s. They are the optimum compromise between being able to spot a target and hold it steady enough from a heaving platform.

Depth-sounders

Although it is often useful to be able to read depths of over 30 fathoms, as for picking up the Labadie Bank on the way back from the Fastnet, say, most yachtsmen primarily want to know how close they are to grounding in shoal water.

The traditional method of heaving a lead is no longer practical or desirable while underway (imagine the chaos of catching the blooper on the let-go), but it remains an unanswerable check against an electronic echo-sounder with the boat at rest, even if your lead line consists of a winch-handle tied on to a spare sheet.

Crewing in RCODs on the Crouch or X-boats in Chichester Harbour we had a stout bamboo cane marked to a length one foot more than the draught of the boat. On orders this dipstick was pushed down on the lee side. A touch meant lee-oh. For small workboats or fishing dayboats I see no harm in that.

But most boats have an electronic echo-sounder pinging through a transducer in the hull with a remote reading display over the chart-table and/or on deck. There are many brands on offer. This is an area where you tend not to get your money's worth, in that some of the cheaper models are better than their more prestigious competitors. A demonstration afloat is the only answer. Find out:

(a) the datum of the depth displayed: e.g. is it measuring from the waterline? the bottom of the keel? or the depth of the transducer below the surface?

It is usually the last, but check. Zero-point on the display can be adjusted to suit. Then have a Dyno strip glued alongside the echo-sounder display saying 'We ground at 1.8m (6ft) on the clock'. Most owners feel comfortable with the actual depth of water displayed, since that is what is on the chart.

A few years ago I went on a blind date navigating an Admiral's Cup boat. Going out from Cowes to the start of the first inshore race I asked where the echo-sounder measured from. No one knew, so the owner abruptly altered to put the boat aground on the Shrape where we could verify the matter by noting the difference between the draft and the depth on the echo-sounder. There was a sluicing ebb tide, so I advised against that plan, thus narrowly avoiding watching the race from a mud berth.

(b) The behaviour of the display in shallow water.

Sometimes it flicks back and forth just when you most need an unambiguous steady reading. Tuning the gain does not always calm it down.

(c) Whether false echoes, like shoals of fish, show up for what they are.

There are all kinds of fancy warning devices on offer, like a hooter to sound off before you ground at anchor on a falling tide. But none is better than the instrument's ability to interpret the raw data.

What present-day yachts' echo-sounders will *not* do is warn you that you are about to hit an underwater obstruction or sudden steep shelving. So it's of little use short-tacking along the Green at Cowes. Nor was there any warning for single-handed circumnavigator Desmond Hampton when *Gipsy Moth V* piled on to an island in the Bass Strait while he slept.

There's no substitute for having a good look at the exposed rocks and foreshore at Low Water Springs and noting your own safe transits. Other people's local knowledge can only be evaluated by trial and error. Uffa Fox often frightened me by urging Max Aitken to take his big wishbone schooner *Lumberjack* ever closer inshore in a foul tide. At one spot his confidence was based on having ridden his mare, Frantic, off the beach and out of her depth at that point. Suddenly we came up all-standing at 10 knots. 'We must have drawn more than 16 hands', was Max's historic comment.

Even apparently up-to-date charts will not be 100% guarantee if depended upon for the last couple of feet under the keel. Approach channels shift (Christchurch, Exmouth and the mouth of the Beaulieu River, for example); harbour entrances silt up (Brighton Marina); underwater obstructions may not always be marked on the chart (Remember the two top British 1985 Admiral's Cup boats which hit the same submerged wreck south of Bembridge Ledge? One of them sank.); unusually low tides can occur after a prolonged blow from one direction, often giving less water over a bar (like Salcombe).

Once I was having a late lunch at Chausey with Marin-Marie the great French marine artist whose flagstaff in front of his waterside home always flew an RORC burgee as an invitation to members dropping anchor there. We had to pick up a crew member at St Helier at a fixed time, so I was anxious to be away. Our host persuaded me to stop for another cognac. The time lost would be recovered by having the local lifeboat coxswain tow us out through the more direct but narrow North channel. Four hours later we were able to walk back to the Hotel du Fort et des Îles for an early dinner, as cows grazed around our keel.

The RORC's log of *Griffin II* on a Morgan Cup Race in 1957 describes how she won the race on a moonless night by short-tacking along the front at Brighton closer inshore than her rivals, cheating the tide. The moment to tack and stand off was not called from the echo-sounder. Instead a crewman on the pulpit hurled an empty bottle ahead as far as he could. If it was heard to hit the shingle on the beach it was time to go about. The race was also memorable when Slushie the Cook was caught dhobying his underpants in the pressure-cooker, having first flashed up the Primus using liqueur brandy instead of methylated spirits. Both worked well – for him.

In bigger boats some go for a stylus display on a moving paper reel, which plots out the shape of the bottom, but is hardly worth the space it takes up.

Of all the modern aids to navigation the echo-sounder remains the least reliable and therefore the one most in need of a corroborative check at any opportunity.

The moral of all these frightening stories of unexpected grounding is that the cruising yachtsman need never put them to the test. Keep outside the 2–fathom (or 3m) line unless you are in a well-buoyed channel and have some idea of the height of the tide above chart datum. For all practical purposes this is Low Water Springs.

Predicting depths

To find out what depth of water there will be at a given time and day in any port, first determine the range of the tides there. This is simply the difference between the heights above datum at HW and LW.

(1) Look up the heights above datum for high and low water, Springs and Neaps. These figures are given at the head of each port covered by the *Shell Pilot to the English Channel* or can be obtained from local tide tables, or by looking up the nearest Standard Port in the almanacs. Take Alderney:

At Springs MHW	6m3	At Neaps MHW	4m7
MLW	om8	MLW	2m6
Range	5m5		2m1 (diff. 3m4)

The progression of the tides from Neaps to Springs is approximately one-seventh for each day after Neaps. If Neaps were on the 17th and we want the range on the 21st, it will be $\frac{4}{7} \times 3m4$ (the difference between Spring and Neap ranges) which is 2mo above Neaps, so the range that day will be 4m1.

(2) Then apply the 'Twelfths Rule' which states that for each successive hour after LW the tide will rise as follows (in twelfths of the range):

$$1 - 2 - 3 - 3 - 2 - 1.$$

So, if LW is at 09.30 and you want to know what the depth will be at noon on the day when the range will be 4m1 it will be found by adding $1 + 2 + 1\frac{1}{2}$ twelfths, or

$$\frac{4 \cdot 5}{12} \times 4.1 = 1m5 \text{ above MLW Neaps (2m1)}$$

which is 3m6 water at noon that day.

You can just as easily work back from HW.

These are only approximations and do not apply where there are double High Waters. For these you should work your way through the prediction-method in the Admiralty form NP159, the curves within almanac tides tables, or rely on locally published tables. No system exists to be more precise after the wind has been blowing strongly for a week in the same direction except to ask the local harbourmaster.

Speed and distance log

For any displacement powerboat or yacht under auxiliary power with her sails furled the simplest way of judging speed made good (Vmg) through the water is to know the rev-knot ratio of the motor. It is usually a straight line relationship (e.g. at 2,000rpm you will be making 7kts, 1,500rpm is $5\frac{1}{4}$kts and 1,000rpm $3\frac{1}{2}$kts). The amount to add or subtract for tidal current is a matter of looking up the relevant tidal information for the place and time of day. Then there is an allowance to be made for windage.

For example, if the chart tells you there should be 1.3kts favourable current and you are motoring before a stiff breeze, make a judgement on how fast you would be going with no motor at all. Unless it is a gale of wind, it is unlikely to be over a knot on top of the tide. Let's say 2kts for tide and wind. The rev-knot ratio says 6kts, so you should be making 8kts over the ground. How much to allow for windage is a matter of observation based on experience of the boat. It is a simple matter to check by timing a run between two known points and working out the distance run, using a calculator or looking it up in a speed-time-distance table. There is a simple formula for doing this without either: the distance a ship runs in hundreds of yards in 3 minutes is its speed in knots, so that 900yds in 3 minutes or 300yds in 1 minute both mean 9kts. This can also be expressed as:

$$\text{Speed in knots} = \frac{\text{distance in yards}}{\text{time in seconds}} \times 1.8$$

$$\text{or:} \qquad = \frac{\text{distance in miles}}{\text{time in minutes}} \times 60$$

$$\text{or:} \qquad = \frac{\text{distance in feet}}{10 \times \text{time in seconds}} \times 6$$

The last lends itself to calculating the speed by using a Dutchman's log, which is by timing how long it takes your boat to sail her own length. The classic way of doing this is to have someone in the pulpit with a few empty beer cans and another in the taffrail with a stopwatch. The first one throws a can out ahead of the boat and far enough out to avoid hitting the hull. As it passes him he drops his hand. The man aft then times the can as it passes the taffrail. This should be repeated to get a mean reading. Thus, sailing a 40ft boat, if a beer can is timed to take 4 seconds to pass down its overall length her speed is:

$$\frac{40 \times 6}{4 \times 10} = 6 \text{ kts}$$

Another aid to judging speed through the water is to use a formula developed by RAF photo-reconnaissance aircraft for measuring ships' speeds. The square root of the distance in feet from the stem to the point where the *second* bow-wave shows against the hull × 1.4 is its speed in knots. With modern yachts this also defines hull speed (up to the threshold of planing), for the second bow-wave is at the transom and holding the boat in a formula:

$$\text{Hull speed} = 1.4\sqrt{\text{length of wetted surface}}$$

Thus a boat 36ft long has a theoretical maximum hull speed of $1.4 \times \sqrt{36} = 1.4 \times 6 = 8.4\text{kts}$.

In calm seas the position of the second bow-wave against the ship's side is clearly seen from on deck. Say the shrouds are 16ft abaft the stem and the leading edge of the cockpit 25ft. Then the second bow-wave abreast these points would be 1.4×4 (5.6kts) and 1.4×5 (7kts) respectively. The beauty of this method is that errors of estimating the distance abaft the stem are square-rooted.

Experienced sailors looking over the side can make a fair guess at the speed of a yacht, probably correct to ±1kt. Powerboats are more difficult, but their shaft rpm/kt ratio is more reliable than any other *ad hoc* method.

I am not suggesting that a log is not one of the Bare Necessities, but simply recalling an era before the advent of reliable hull-mounted logs when Erroll Bruce and Adlard Coles persuaded us after their epic Transatlantic Race in 24ft sloops that a towed log over that distance could add $8\frac{1}{2}$ hours to the elapsed time of a 6-kt passage even if it only slowed you down by 0.1kt. So for the next few seasons many RORC navigators kept their towed logs inboard and used variations of the methods spelled out above.

On balance I believe a reliable log is a highly desirable comfort to the navigator. Some, like the Walker towed log, primarily reel off distance run. The paddle wheel or impeller type, like B & G, primarily read speed. But either can be used as the prime source for giving the other dimension on a remote analogue or digital display.

Towed logs are appreciably cheaper than any electronic models. The correct way to stream one is to pay out the inboard end of the rope first, so as to get all the kinks out of it. Then recover it hand over hand, hook on and let the spinner trail aft. The snags are:

(a) Some fish take them as bait, usually snapping the line. So you must carry a spare.

(b) You must remember to hand the log before entering harbour or shoal water, before going astern on the motor, or towing a dinghy or crossing another yacht astern.

(c) Unless you have a remote reading dial, you have to get to the taffrail to take readings.

(d) They can be fouled by weed, especially in tropical waters. Or they can snag a J-cloth or other gash finding its way overboard.

There is also available an electronic trailing log which does not spin on its own tow-line, but transmits the rotation of a helical impeller as speed and distance to analogue dials inboard.

Impeller logs are extremely accurate, provided they have been calibrated, adjusted and checked to lie in the same plane as the water flowing under the hull. After calibration by checking over a measured distance in tideless conditions (or by taking the average of runs in reciprocal directions), the display reading for speed and distance can be adjusted by a thumb-screw on the back of the display console. My general experience is that it pays not to adjust the log unless you have piled up a mass of evidence in favour of doing so. Then do it in very small steps.

The location of impellers can be critical, so it is as well to take technical advice from the suppliers if you are fitting one

Cap to be screwed on to hull fitting when impeller is inboard

Withdraw

unscrew before pulling impeller inboard

Weed trap

for the first time. You want to be in undisturbed waterflow, free from surface aeration or coming clear of the water when pitching. In bigger boats it is the practice to fit two impellers, with a gravity switch changing from port to starboard automatically on tacking.

To adjust for optimum reading, slack off the cap locking the log and have someone watch on the display unit to see what happens when you slew the impeller slowly from 15° off centreline, through fore-and-aft to 15° off the other way. When the reading peaks at highest speed, lock the impeller. It will not always be precisely in the fore-and-aft line, especially if the hull-mounting is off-centre. With two impellers you find that both are toed slightly inwards. This is a very sensitive adjustment.

Likewise it is important to have the impeller pushed downwards to its full extent.

Although modern impeller logs have much improved fore-and-aft weedguards, they are still prone to pick up foreign bodies.

On sailing into kelp or a cluster of *Sargassum* weed trouble soon manifests itself, as the log suddenly stops recording.

Last summer I gathered a collector's item 20 miles south of Anvil Point. The log was stopped by a condom of such heroic proportions that we had a lively debate whether it had come overboard from a Russian or American ship. But even fine strands of weed can wrap themselves in the bearing of the impeller and slow it down, so that the boat-speed may drop only imperceptibly, giving rise to sidelong glances at the helmsman or talk of a sail-change.

In either case the remedy is the same – an awkward, wet job for the navigator. First the sailbags and off-watch oilskins have to be yanked clear before the impeller can be withdrawn into the boat and the hull-fitting shut off by screwing its cap on. Fine weed is best removed by a winkle-pin. To check it is clear, puff at the impeller to ensure it is spinning freely and activating the display dial. If it whizzes round and does not show on the dial, you have a real problem – maybe a fault in the cable run.

But it may be more serious. Ten days out from the Canaries in a Swan '47', rolling along the 17th parallel in a steady 25kt breeze from the quarter against a blue-and-white backdrop of breaking seas and marching cumulus, we celebrated our furthest point from land with a tot of Fundador. We were nowhere near any shipping lane and hadn't seen anything but seabirds and flying-fish for over a week. Suddenly there was a loud bang. A whale or a submerged oil drum perhaps? Then a 4in plank about 10ft long surfaced in our wake. To be more precise, two 5ft planks did, neatly bisected by a karate chop from our stem. The log now read zero. Both impellers had been sheared off clean, weedguards and all. No more flotsam was seen, then or for the rest of the trip, so we must have picked up a solitary paint-ship plank which could have fallen overboard off Lisbon or Bantry Bay.

Set approximately 1m apart, the Sonic Speed transducers operate outside the boundary layer on the centre-line of the boat

Paddlewheel Logs Most logs these days are of the paddlewheel variety which are less prone to be fouled by weed. Their installation should follow the same guidelines as for impeller logs.

The Sonic Log A new log which defies all underwater debris because its two sensors are flush-fitted to the hull is the Brookes & Gatehouse sonic log. This measures the difference between the speed of sound at rest and that at any boat-speed, by averaging out the different timing of signals pulsing alternately fore-and-aft.

The location of the transducers is critical: on the centre-line not less than 2ft 6in (0.8m) or more than 4ft 6in (1.4m) apart and set at an angle of 20°–30° below the horizontal. This requirement makes the log suitable only for boats with fin keels. The usual arrangement is to have the forward transducer about 3ft forward of the point of attachment of the keel to the hull and the after one 2ft down its leading edge. For measuring speed through the water it seems to be the complete answer.

Other means of measuring speed and distance run Most of the hyperbolic aids (Decca, Loran-C, for example) have built-in computers which will provide all the speed-and-distance answers by working out solutions between successive fixes. But they have their own aberrations which will be discussed later in the book. Even farther out of reach for yachtsmen because of cost and/or weight are certain military toys, like the Global Position System – a continuous-fixing Sat-Nav – or the Inertial Navigation System as fitted in nuclear submarines. There is also the eternal dream of a doppler log which will give course and speed made good over the seabed. But no one has yet cracked that as a practical proposition for yachtsmen.

The Bare Necessities – Good enough for 'Suhaili' On his epic 27,000 mile solo circumnavigation lasting 313 days in 1968/9 Robin Knox-Johnston managed on:

* a magnetic compass of the same type as fitted in a ship's lifeboat, with an old ex-Service hand-bearing compass as stand-by
* a hand lead line
* celestial navigation tables and an old sextant whose mirrors were soon blotched by seawater
* a wind-up chronometer depending for its credibility on time signals from his radio
* only 13 Admiralty charts, because he couldn't afford more even in those far-off days when they cost half a guinea each. Some of them were stamped 'Not to be used for navigation'
* parallel rulers, dividers and pencils
* a towed log, which he gave up using after it was fouled in the Doldrums by gooseneck barnacles, which look like toothpaste and cling like limpets. So he made over 20,000 miles without a log.

More recently Dr Marvin Creamer has made a leisurely circumnavigation in a 35ft boat without any navigation aids whatever – not even a clock – and won the CCA's 1985 Blue Water Medal for it, but that merely demonstrates what Drake and Magellan had to do, not what is recommended for you or the couple heading from Hamble to the upper reaches of the Thames. Dr Creamer knew he'd rounded the Horn by hitting neither the land nor the ice.

Even in the smallest yachts I hold that space and thought devoted to providing the navigator with an efficiently designed and equipped chart-table will pay dividends. In today's parlance this tends to be called 'the nav-station', but it means the same thing: a corner where the navigator can do his work with the least distraction and yet within easy communication of the helmsman.

If you are buying a stock boat you have to take what is already installed and then fit in all the navigator's aids to his best advantage.

If you are building or converting then you might do better. The following considerations apply:

(a) *Location* In a powerboat with a cabin there is no problem: the chart-table should be a working surface next to the wheel facing for'ard. The worst chart-table I ever endured was the attack-plot in an 'H' Class submarine (vintage 1916). When the attack team was closed up, my station was sitting inside the head, with the door shut and its upper panel pulled down on to my knees as the plotting surface. Once, I left the tools of my trade elsewhere, so the straight edge of a toothbrush handle was conscripted as a substitute for dividers and protractors. It seemed to work, but luckily it was not in the face of the enemy.

No frills on this single screw powerboat

Single screw powerboat layout. Chart-table inaccessible

Clock **Kent clear-view screens** **Barometer**

Speed log

Echo-sounder

Radar

Engine dials

Chart table

Radio telephone

Typical powerboat layout with chart-table folded out of use

In a yacht without a wheel-house there are many options. My worst memories centre on the Ron Holland Two-Tonner *Knockout*, when the chart-table was set fore-and-aft against the ship's side, opposite the galley – some distance from the hatch leading to the cockpit. On one tack the working surface was far below me and heeled away at 25°. On the other there was little to stop everything ending up in the galley bilge. On top of that, the cabin sole had to be kept clear for stowing sailbags amidships and for moving them when required. So the navigator's seat was a round stool-top on a swinging arm which could be stowed out of the way under the chart-table.

That experience need not rule out a fore-and-aft chart-table altogether. For example if you have a narrow shoal-draught boat with a high centreboard casing dividing the available space below in half, there may be no alternative. Such is the case in a Freedom 34 which John Oakeley swears by (see p. 43). He has deliberately put his chart-table well forward and away from the hatch so as to keep sea and rain off his electronics. In practical terms most electronic nav-aids are in splash-proof consoles, so the principal sufferers from water coming down the hatch are the charts and the navigator himself.

A fore-and-aft table is also acceptable in any boat which is designed to be sailed upright, like a multi-hull. Otherwise the choice must be overwhelmingly for an athwartships working surface near the after hatch.

In *Toscana* (ex-*Blizzard*, the Frers '51' IOR prototype) the chart-table was once amidships, permitting the navigator the luxury of a tilting seat which could be locked at an angle when the boat was heeled. Not so good for short-tacking. The trouble with this arrangement was that anything not nailed down to the table had two ways in which to go when the boat gave a lurch.

So we end up with the solution most often found in stock boats: a nav-station built out from the ship's side with the after cabin bulkhead forming the backrest to the navigator's seat.

The all-time best nav-station for me was in the 48ft Illingworth & Primrose cutter *Outlaw*. The navigator worked facing aft, with a rectangular port at eye level through which he could communicate with the helmsman, since the wheel was on the bulkhead at the for'ard end of the cockpit. The helmsman could look straight down on to his chart, while the navigator and skipper both had quarter-berths in the after cabin, shut off from the rest of the boat (see p. 44).

Barometer

Calculator

Deviation Form

Syma 4000 Automatic Direction Finding Unit

Icom M.80 Radio

Radar

Travacrest System (Boat speed, Wind speed/Angle, Heading, Depth, Log, etc)

Lokata Watchman Radar Detector

RS 4000 Decca Set

Centreboard casing

A connoisseur's Nav-Station.
Sir John Oakeley's 'Freedom'

43

'OUTLAW' (1963) navigator-helmsman communications
Helmsman has compass and full range of B & G dials in front of him. All sail trimming is abaft him and does not distract.

(b) *Vital Statistics* The working surface of the chart-table should be at least big enough to take an Admiralty chart folded once, say 30in × 22in. The navigator's seat should have 18in lateral clearance abaft the table, with a bench height of 19in and a least clearance under the bottom of the chart-table structure of 8in. The lid of the chart-table should be hinged at its forward end with a least depth of 4in of stowage under it. Thus the ideal height of the chart-table working surface should be 32in. The top should be flat and contained within the fiddles 1in proud on each side; across its after side either a $\frac{1}{2}$in fiddle or provision for spring-steel clips to hold the chart in position. The lid should be hinged so as to open to at least 45° and be held there either by an overhead shockcord or by a prop.

Under one end of the chart stowage there should be a drawer not less than 4in × 4in section to accommodate the spare pencils, rubbers, pencil sharpener, stopwatch, the keys for locking up the boat, a mini-torch and lens cleaning paper.

The open end of the navigator's seat must be provided with a click-on safety harness strong enough to take his full weight when heeled.

(c) *Lighting* All the boat's lighting down below should ideally have red or white optional bulbs, preferably of the type activated by twisting their glass shades either way. Additionally the chart-table should have its own flexible finger-light so arranged that it can, if need be, illuminate the inside of the chart-table when its lid is open. Red lighting below should be the norm for the crew, but the navigator must have the luxury of a white finger-light for chartwork, provided it does not catch the helmsman's eye.

During the Transatlantic Race in 1960 in *Drumbeat* we got dismasted around the change of the watch at midnight. At the cry for 'all hands on deck' all the cabin lighting was switched on – white. As they stumbled out on deck one or two of

Cruising yacht lay-out

the crew nearly went straight over the side, reaching for guardwires which were no longer there. They were not acclimatized to night vision, as they would have been if they had rolled out of their racks into red lighting.

Tools of the trade There must be secure stowages for pencils, dividers, parallel ruler or protractor, a rubber, the navigator's spectacles (or a magnifying glass) and the almanacs or tables in use.

The last needs a bookrack capable of holding publications 11in × 8in so arranged that they don't fly out at any angle of heel. It should be 18in long, but can be split into two.

Nav-Station in a First '32'

Decca Navigator
Lokata radio D/F set
B & G Log & Speed
Finger-light
Barometer
Spare Compass
Ship's electrics board
Echo-sounder
Engine switchboard
Navigator's harness

Inside the chart-table the charts needed for the passage should be placed in the order in which they are going to be used, with a small-scale general chart of the whole voyage on top. All the rest of the charts should be stowed elsewhere, possibly in an 'envelope', as they call those linen-backed chart folders, or a plastic cover and put under the mattress of the navigator's bunk.

Unless there is some ruthless weeding out, the chart-table will be the crew's receptacle for their car keys, dark glasses, wallets, pop tapes, old sailing instructions, girlie magazines, spare batteries, sheath-knives and various technical manuals. My first move on joining for a trip is to clear the chart-table of everything of this nature into a bin-liner and stow it in the heads.

Other designed stowages within easy reach of the chart-table should be provided. Here I admit that we are moving on from the bare necessities to include many nav-aids commonly found in cruising or racing boats:

Hand-bearing compass
Binoculars
D/F antenna and headset
Sextant

Radar
VHF radio-telephone
Chart-table finger-light
R D/F battery portable
Electrical panel
Echo-sounder
Engine dials
Brookes & Gatehouse Hornet digital presentation
Chart stowage under

Nav-Station in a 34ft yacht

Also located so that the navigator can see or operate them without moving should be:

The electrical switchboard, with the navigator and mast-head lights on separate switches, a switch to illuminate the steering compass with an accompanying dimmer rheostat, the engine starting-switch and a voltmeter to interrogate the batteries before and during charging
Echo-sounder display
Log-speed console and display
Wind direction and velocity displays
Any hyperbolic aid (Decca or Loran-C) or Sat-Nav.
Radio telephone
A simple pocket calculator fixed to a bulkhead for dealing with speed-time-distance problems
More sophisticated calculators, which can go all the way to replacing every nautical table and solve celestial navigation problems, are best kept in the chart-table drawer.
Ship's clock
Barometer
Spare compass unit
High-intensity torch and/or Aldis light for signalling.

Given the above the navigator can readily monitor the yacht's progress. He should be situated so that it is simple to get his head-and-shoulders into the hatch to take bearings or verify any shore features by visual confirmation. He would be well advised to have his own pocket torch and binoculars.

The Cruise Director
The navigator has more to do than seeing that the right charts are on board and getting the boat from A to B. He should also act as hotel manager to the skipper, especially in a boat carrying more than 4 in the crew. The general plan of the voyage or race should be displayed on a small sketch,

explained to the crew before departure and kept up-to-date. Thus a voyage from the Hamble to St Malo would show the courses and distances on the 5 legs of the trip: West Solent – Needles – Casquets – Les Hanois – SW Minquiers buoy – Le Grand Jardin. The plan will show courses and distances, the times of HW and the duration of the ebb and flow of each tide.

Also displayed for the duration of the voyage is the watch-list and routine to be followed. Yachtsmen argue endlessly about the best system to be employed. There's a lot to be said for the Royal Navy system of 4-hour watches with split 2-hour dog watches in the evenings (to avoid the same watch doing the Middle every night). A 1230 turnover at the end of the forenoon watch ensures that lunch is not eaten too early. A popular variation of that is to keep two 6-hour watches by day and three 4-hour ones at night. It depends on the weather, the number of competent helmsmen in each watch and the degree of concentration called for. In submarines we stood watches on a straight 2-on 4-off rota. One advantage claimed is that a maximum of $3\frac{1}{2}$ hours in the sack at any time keeps watchkeepers more alert and in the tactical picture. Whichever system is adopted the navigator should keep an eye on seeing that the watches are called, fed and relieved on time. Nothing saps morale quicker than sloppiness in this area. Washing-up, keeping the bilges low and the batteries topped up should also be the subject of timely reminders from the nav-station.

On a long voyage in easy conditions a 3-watch system is desirable, even if you only have a crew of 3. Be ready to go to 2 watches if the weather turns sour. Alternatively have an extra offwatch hand on call, snoozing under cover in oilskins and safety harness.

The navigator must catch the weather reports and handle any compulsory race-reporting by R/T. There are views about weather broadcasts, since their predictions are by no means infallible. Too often they lead to unwise early or late sail changes or holding too far off rhumb-line in anticipation of a wind-shift. Rod Stephens never allowed his crews to listen to weather forecasts for those reasons. My view is that the shipping forecasts should be respected before setting out on a cruise or passage but, once at sea, it is best to keep an eye on the barometer, the clouds and the behaviour of the wind. The weather you have to deal with is here and now, not what some aspiring TV pundit has to say from the London Weather Centre.

The weather actuals are often a better indication of what is to come than the area forecasts (see Chap. 8).

Also on display in the nav-station should be the complete sail inventory, with areas, cloth weights, limit of wind speeds, sheeting positions for each sail. Each sail-bag and its normal stowage should be indicated by an abbreviated designation, as shown below:

Log-books

It is perfectly possible to make local passages without the formality of recording them, but even when not racing, it is vital for the navigator to keep an accurate deck-log if the voyage is out of sight of land, overnight or in poor visibility. In the Royal Navy and many merchantmen two logs are kept: a deck-log, entered in pencil by the OOW or quartermaster, recording events as they happened; and a Fair Log, written in ink from the deck-log and in due course forwarded to the Admiralty or the shipping line's head office.

A misdemeanour by an officer, short of meriting a court-martial, would be entered in the Fair Log in red ink and signed by the commanding officer at an uncomfortable ceremony at a table with a green baize cloth. 'I had occasion this day to reprimand Lieutenant O'Hare for his negligent handling of HM Ship under my Command during close manoeuvres on the screen.' Meaning: Mick ordered the wheel to port on executing a Blue 18 turn and missed cutting Captain (D)'s ship in two by a coat of paint. This procedure was known as 'logging'. In a well-organized wardroom this page would then be used for lighting a cigar and a new one inserted before forwarding it to Their Lordships. Since they ended up unopened in a warehouse in North London, no harm was done.

Bag No.	Colour	Sail	Area	Weight	Max Wind	Stowed	Sheeting
H 1	red band	Heavy No. 1 Genoa	900	11	33	forepeak stb aft	23 inboard
SP 1	green	Max. spinnaker	1600	1.5	18	Nav bunk	Quarter blocks
TRI	white	Storm trisail	350	17	60	Pt fr'd cockpit	Boom end

Some merchant navy Fair Logs were taken very seriously indeed. The Blue Funnel Line used to require all chartwork to be plotted over courses marked up ashore beforehand in Indian ink. Every chart used during the voyage had to be forwarded to head office for scrutiny by the Marine Superintendent. These were compared with the Fair Logs to ensure that neither had been cooked and that the company's routing policy (10 miles off most headlands and always within two days' steaming of the nearest other Blue Funnel ship) had been observed. Officers' promotion depended partly on not deviating from these guidelines. The company thus saved millions on insurance and salvage.

Happily no such standards are required of yacht navigators, but, apart from their nostalgic value, they are invaluable in the never-ending process of knowing where you are. Time and again it is necessary to reconstruct your plot. Without a reliable deck-log you might as well be blindfold. As for logging foredeck hands for their behaviour ashore in St Malo or Santander, forget it.

Like protractors and parallel rulers the best format is what you are used to. There are many log-books available from chandleries. Most of them are too big or too inflexible for my taste.

I rely on the Imray Laurie Norris and Wilson Navigator's Log Book. It is a loose-leaf book between solid splashproof plastic covers: measuring $10\frac{1}{2}$in across by 7in deep, so fits neatly into the standard bookshelf above. By unscrewing two brass bolts, extra pages can be added. Or, before a long trip, all the previously used pages can be taken out and stowed out of harm's way.

Each page is ruled off with a narrow column on its left (for the time of each entry) a generous space for describing the relevant event and five more narrow columns on the right. None is designated. So start by doing so, adding extra column(s) as may be needed:

Time	Voyage from Cowes to Plymouth Remarks	Bar	Log	Tuesday 14th August 1979 Co	Sp	Wind
0005	Down to 2 reefs, small staysail	990	37.9	315	8	SSW8
0040	JR out on boom to reeve off last reef	986	59.0	285	8	SSW9
0235	Fastnet bg 280	980	59.0	285	8	SSW9
0345	Tacked to port on parting jib sheet	980	65.1	280	8	W9
0504	Fastnet abm to port	980	73.5	190	9	W9
0636	*Marionette* lying a-hull. No assistance needed. Listened out on Ch.16. First inkling of scale of problem	982	86.2	135	9	WNW9
1045	Call cookie at 11.30 50 miles from Rock av 8.9kts	994	723.5	135	9	WNW8

Those are extracts from the log of the Swan '47' *Toscana*. The 'JR' who walked along the boom to reeve off the third slab was none other than John Rousmaniere whose subsequent book *Fastnet – Storm 10* is a classic.

Note:

(a) Times are local (BST)

(b) Remarks are as they were written at the height of the storm

(c) The normal practice of hourly or half-hourly entries was abandoned during the horrendous $2\frac{1}{2}$-hour battle to get round the Rock against the new 30ft WNW seas building over the old SSW swell

(d) Barometer readings have been added as an extra column. The fall of 10 mbs in $2\frac{1}{2}$h spelled real trouble – as if we needed telling.

(e) Only the last two digits of the log reading are entered.

(f) The course and speed entered are those which the helmsman reported having averaged since the previous entry. Note: courses ordered and steered are always to the nearest 5° magnetic, on the assumption that no one can sail an intermediate course with confidence. These are invaluable, not only in concentrating the helmsman's mind, but for manual plotting as a check against other aids (we were outside Loran-C cover, had no Decca or Sat-Nav).

(g) The winds entered are supposed to be their true direction and strength on the Beaufort Scale. Since then I have decided to enter them as Magnetic and their velocity in knots, since that is how we read them off instruments and relate to the ordered course.

(h) In other circumstances, such as Gulf Stream sailing, an extra column is added to record seawater temperatures.

The left-hand facing page is blank. On this race I find much useful information has been added there. On the first page all legs of the race are listed, giving course and distances for each:

Leg	Co(T)	Dist(nm)
Start-Hurst Pt	252°	11
Needles-Anvil Pt	255°	19
Anvil Pt-Start Pt	259°	70
Start Pt-Lizard	264°	63
Lizard-Runnelstone	290°	18
Runnelstone-Longships	323°	5
Longships-Fastnet	310°	168
Fastnet-Bishop	136°	151
Bishop-Lizard	094°	48
Lizard-Rame	068°	$46\frac{1}{2}$
Total		$599\frac{1}{2}$

HW Dover BST	Sat 1406	Sun 0231
		1452
HW Devonport BST		Sun 0954
		2210

The last page of that log recorded the defects:

$\frac{3}{4}$ oz spinnaker blown out
No. 4 Genoa boltrope ripped out
Top 3 main battens need replacing
After heads U/S
Stb bow light flooded
Man overboard light shorted out
1 jib sheet parted

And it summed up the end of the race:

Finished at 15.23.59 close astern of *Midnight Sun*, ahead of *Matrero* and *Alliance*. Secured Mill Bay Dock alongside *Uinna-mara*.

Sailed 631 miles in 97hrs 14mins. Av 6.49kts (6.15kts on rhumb line)

Logged 665 miles; 5% over-log accounted by adverse balance of tides encountered.

The log of taking the boat over to English Harbour subsequently in a strictly cruise mode with three watches of two each makes different reading. The menu for each meal is recorded on the left-hand page, while a periodic muster of consumables is all recorded. Ten days out from Puerto Rico at the southern tip of Gran Canarias, we recorded the following (figures in brackets indicate consumption so far):

Vino blanco	9 (13)
Tinto	18 (14)
Vodka	2 (5)
Scotch	3 (1)
La Ina	3 ($\frac{1}{2}$)
Rum	$2\frac{1}{2}$(4)
Brandy	$1\frac{1}{2}$($\frac{1}{2}$)
Port	$1\frac{1}{4}$($\frac{3}{4}$)

'Discounting secret supplies'

Five days later we were down to 22 gallons of fuel, 5 bottles of vino, $\frac{3}{4}$ 'non-Gallic' cognac and 1 sherry, but hadn't hit the Scotch. The log recorded Devil's Island as the nearest point of land, 945 miles away. Concorde's double boom was noted on its way from Caracas to Paris. 'Hands to bathe', each 1,000

miles from the Canaries and distances left to run were logged. And so on until anchoring in Freeman's Bay 17 days 2hrs 40mins out, having made good 7.05kts for 2,895 miles at 169 miles per day.

It's all in the Log-book.

The Ship's Book

An invaluable addition to the navigator's bookshelf is a loose-leaf reference book containing all the data needed to operate the boat efficiently, especially those needed at short notice. It should include:

- Times and heights of HW Dover. Any local tide tables.
- The sail inventory, stowages and sheeting positions
- The compass deviation card.
- Photostat of latest IOR, IMS or Channel rating certificates.
- Photostat of Ship's Papers and docking plan.
- Speed/r.p.m. table under power.
- Dutchman's log table.
- Table of breakeven speeds whilst reaching off.
- Sources of weather forecasts: frequencies and telephone numbers.
- Safety equipment check-list, giving stowages and dates of last certification.
- Extracts or digests from all the technical manuals covering the boat's machinery and electronics.
- Crew roster, names, addresses and telephone numbers for homes and offices. Next-of-kin particulars.
- Useful addresses and telephone numbers: boat yard, designer, sail-maker, yacht clubs, chart suppliers, taxis, restaurants, etc.

Chart conventions and symbols

Times are expressed in four figures as shown on a 24-hour clock. Thus 9 p.m. is 2100 – not 21.00 hours – just 2100. Sometimes a suffix may be added to indicate the Time Zone which the ship's clock is keeping. The 15° straddling our Greenwich meridian – that is from 07°30W to 07°30E – is where Greenwich Mean Time rules. It carries the suffix 'Z'. If British Summer Time is in force the Navy carries the suffix 'A', but it is less confusing to add in brackets the correction needed to adjust to GMT. Thus 1300Z (or GMT) becomes 1400(−1) during British Summer Time.

Sailing in NW European waters you soon find out that all our neighbours except the Micks keep their clocks an hour ahead of us. So 1615(−1) in Chichester will be the same time as 1715(−2) in Cherbourg. It is a point to remember when looking up the times of tides, ferry departures or banking hours.

For each 15° band of longitude the clock lags one hour behind GMT to the west and keeps one hour ahead to the east. This ensures that the clock times of daylight are approximately the same on any given latitude. 07°30W to 22°30W is Zone +1 on GMT, while 22°30W to 37°30W is Zone +2, and so on.

If you fly out to Hong Kong or even Long Island Sound to navigate a yacht, the first thing to do is make sure you know which Time Zone you are in. All celestial navigation tables and almanacs are based on GMT. Fortunately the BBC World Service resolutely adheres to GMT, so you can pick up its time signal at least once an hour. All local time signals are listed in the almanacs or the *Admiralty List of Radio Signals*.

My tip is: keep a spare clock or wristwatch on GMT all the time. For practical purposes when putting a position on the chart just use the four figures of ship's time.

Distances should always be expressed in nautical miles and decimal fractions. It is fortunate that there are 10 cables (each of 200 yds) in a nautical mile. Thus 4.3nm is 4miles 3cables (600yds). Until the bureaucrats in Brussels insist on charts using kilometres, do all your chartwork and planning in nautical miles. Some illogical quirks are already creeping in. Our Met Office expresses visibility in its shipping forecasts in nautical miles, until it falls below a mile, when they suddenly talk of metres. Distances should be read off the vertical scale of latitudes at the side of the chart at or near the latitude you are in. All digital logs present their information in nautical miles and two places of decimals.

Heights and depths are increasingly quoted in metres to a single place of decimal. Just remember that 1.8 metres, usually written 1m8 or shown on a chart as 1_8 is 6ft: That is 1 fathom, which may be more familiar. Unless otherwise stated, the notional height of a navigational light is expressed in metres, while its visibility range is given in nautical miles. They are distinguished from one another by a small 'm' for metres and a capital 'M' for miles. So a light shown as 15m25M is 15 metres above sea level with a visibility range of 25 miles.

The characteristics of lights and how they are abbreviated have also undergone a change during the recent adoption of metric charts. The descriptions of coastal features are mostly self-evident, such as an estuary is now shown as 'est' whereas formerly it was 'esty'. But the lights themselves need a mild degree of acclimatization. Here are the main ones, with their former designation in brackets:

Oc is a single occulting light, which means a light showing more light than dark (Occ).

Oc (2) shows two short dark breaks in each cycle. Formerly GpOcc(2).

Iso is a new one, with equal light and dark periods.

Fl is a flashing light with less light than dark; not to be confused with F, which is a fixed light.

Fl(3) is a pattern of 3 flashes of light broken by longer periods of dark, used to be shown as GpFl(3). In all cases the duration of each cycle is shown as '20s', meaning 20 seconds from start to finish of each cycle, formerly written as 'ev 20secs'. This is the key one to put your stopwatch on when making a positive identification of a new light just raised.

Q replaces the old QkFl for a light which flashes between 50 and 70 times per minute, so that it has the appearance of a rapid blinker. Even quicker flashers – 80/159 times a minute – are VQ. And there is a rarely seen UQ, which is the Ultra Quick flashing light. Another rare bird is the light which flashes its identity in a continuous repetition of a morse letter. That is Mo(K) for a light which flashes − · − all the time. The colours of lights are self-evident. If not otherwise stated they are white lights. Sometimes they are mixed, when they may be AltWG, which means an alternating white and green light. A WG light is one showing white and green in different sectors at the same time.

IALA buoyage systems

The whole of NW Europe has now conformed with the lights and buoyage system (A) introduced by the International Association of Lighthouse Authorities (IALA) over the past decade. It embraces all the new chart notations mentioned above and elsewhere in this book. It is logical and consistent. The complaint most frequently heard is that the new G flashing lights on all conical starboard-hand buoys – that is ones to be left to starboard on your way in from seaward – are not as easy to pick up as the old W flashers. Many have been intensified recently, but they remain a problem against the background of shore traffic signals and starboard bow-lights in ships under way. Buoys and marks to be left to starboard have odd numbers, starting with No.1 at the outer end of the channel. The port-hand ones have even numbers.

It is important to remember that the cardinal marks (all B and Y) tell you on which side it is safe to pass. There is logic about their topmarks and lights:

N-cardinal mark has two triangular topmarks pointing upwards (i.e. towards the N Pole)

S-cardinal mark has its topmarks pointing downwards, towards the S Pole.

W-cardinal topmarks (apex-to-apex) make a letter 'W' on its side, telling you that it is safe to pass to the west

E-cardinal topmarks (base-to-base) from the Greek letter 'E' – deep water is to the eastward

Even their light characteristics are logical, going in clockwise order from:

N-cardinal – one quick flash
E-cardinal – QFl(3)
S-cardinal – QFl(6)
W-cardinal – QFl(9).

North America – IALA System

North America has a longer coastline that Europe and many thousands of inland waterways governed by different State and Federal authorities, besides the US Coast Guard. So it is not surprising that they have lagged behind the rest of the world in introducing the new IALA system. Instead they have an interim one of their own which features G can buoys with odd numbers (!) and G lights to be left to port on the way up-channel, with R buoys and R lights to be left to starboard.

IALA BUOYAGE

Cardinal Marks

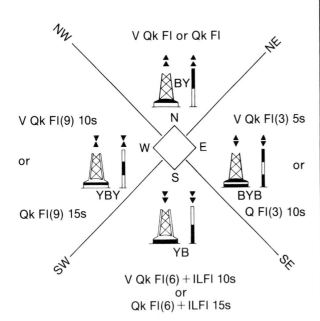

V Qk Fl or Qk Fl

BY

N

V Qk Fl(9) 10s

or

Qk Fl(9) 15s

YBY

W

E

S

V Qk Fl(3) 5s

or

Q Fl(3) 10s

BYB

YB

V Qk Fl(6)+lLFl 10s
or
Qk Fl(6)+lLFl 15s

Buoys indicate safe side of a danger
on which to pass

Lateral Marks

Can topmark

R

Lt R – any
rhythm

Direction
up-channel
from seaward

Cone topmark

G

Lt G – any
rhythm

to mark sides of navigable channels

Other Marks

R & W
SAFE WATER MARKS
Sph topmark
Lt W Iso, Occ or 1 LFl
ev 10s

2 B sph topmarks
Lt W Gp Fl (2)

BRB
ISOLATED DANGER
MARKS
safe water all round

Y   Lt Y

SPECIAL MARKS
not for navigation
X topmark

USA CHANNEL BUOYS

Lateral aids seen from seaward

Port
Odd numbers

G Lt Fl Q Fl
Oc or Iso

Fl G

G

CAN

DAYMARK
G

safe water mid-channels or fairways
no numbers – may be lettered
Lt: FlW (Mo 'A')

RW   RW

RW

Preferred channel
no numbers – may be lettered
Lt: Gp Fl (2 + 1)

Preferred Channel to Stb.

Preferred channel to Port

G
R

R
G

Starboard
Even numbers

R Lt: Fl Q Fl
Oc or Iso

Fl R

R

NUN
R

DAYMARK
R

US MODIFIED IALA 'B' SYSTEM

SPECIAL MARKS

Y UNLIT Y

FlY

Lit

Y

UNTIL 1990 YOU MAY STILL SEE:
REMEMBER: RED RIGHT RETURNING

G or W   BW   R or W

Mid Channel

G or W   R or W

Preferred channel
Lt: Int Q Fl

Port B   stb. R

These include truncated R conical buoys always referred to as 'nuns', as opposed to their G opposite numbers known as 'cans'. Safe channels are R and W, while Preferred channels (a sensible category rarely seen in Europe) are R and G.

But generations of N American sailors have been brought up on **'Red Right Returning'**, their hallowed system still in widespread use. This features B buoys with G or W lights to port and R buoys (R or W lights) or unlit R nuns to starboard. Mid-channel buoys are R and W, while preferred channels are R and B.

Courses and bearings are always expressed in three figures as degrees True. Thus 5° off True North is expressed as 005°. The old cardinal points are never used except in conversation, when they must be assumed to be Magnetic (e.g. SE is S45E, NW is N45W). But the habit of describing a 'point' for about 10° (actually 11¼°) dies hard, for example in saying that a ship has been sighted two points on the port (or starboard) bow.

Elsewhere in this book I have urged navigators to **Think True** – that is to convert all bearings and courses from Magnetic to True before plotting them. When in doubt, the suffix 'T' or 'M' should be added, but it is far easier to carry the approximate compass correction in one's mind and apply it at source. In most yachts this means just the Variation.

Arcs of lights are expressed in degrees True from seaward. Thus the white sector of a light may be shown as 030°–330°, which means that it flashes white 30° either side of North True when observed from seaward.

Plotting and fixing

The prime function of anyone responsible for navigating a boat is to maintain an accurate plot giving an up-dated EP at all times. The EP is the Estimated Position as opposed to the DR (Dead Reckoning). The EP takes account of tide, leeway and windage. Every position I mark on a chart has one of the following notations against its time and log reading:

Fix, meaning spot on, either by virtue of visual bearings or a reliable celestial shot yielding a small cocked hat. Strictly speaking, the latter is an Observed Position (Obs-Pos.) but 'fix' is mostly used. It is the navigator's banker marked on the chart by a dot in a circle (⊙), which can be relied upon after the fog has set in. Sailing *Roundabout* back from Copenhagen after the One-Ton Cup in 1966 I left a guest artist on the tiller after clearing the roads off Copenhagen. Around 0500 I awoke to realize that we were hard aground and in thick fog. There had not been a single entry in the log or on the chart for 4 hours, so it was anyone's guess where we had fetched up. We backed off and sailed a reciprocal course until we picked up an identifiable navigational landmark, but it was a creepy feeling.

DR is the boat's Dead Reckoning position arrived at by simply plotting the course steered and the distance run according to the log. It is indicated by a cross (+).

EP is the boat's Estimated position after allowing for all the known variables. Its accuracy depends on the navigator's input of the variables. It is a lot more reliable than the DR, which is what most yacht navigators tend to plot. It should be shown by a dot inside a triangle (△).

Nowadays most skippers think their electronic nav-aids do away with the need to keep a meticulous EP. All I can say to that proposition is that in the last 20 years of navigating yachts equipped with the most sophisticated nav-aids that money can buy (or the rules of racing permit) I have never yet completed a season without having to fall back on the EP plot. Ah-So (the Japanese computer-assisted read-out from Loran-C or Decca) sometimes chucks his hand in, with blinking amber or red lights telling the navigator he is on his own.

That is why so many boats on the Bermuda Race fail to hit off the NE Breakers buoy on the nose. Indeed, it is not unheard-of for million-dollar IOR boats to miss the island altogether.

If you aspire to be a Royal Navy submarine skipper you may be comforted by the thought that SINS (Submarine Inertial Navigation System, a complex three-dimensional system of highly accurate gyros monitoring the deviation from True North) is designed to give your position at all times accurately enough to hit Colonel Gaddafi's sauna-bath at a range of 2,500 miles. But the hard-nosed Perisher Teacher in charge of the qualifying course makes it his business to find out how you get along without SINS. He gives each pupil a 12-hour spell dived in Inchmarnock Water in the confined approaches to the Clyde without access to any nav-aids other than the compass, the rev-knot table and the echo-sounder. The periscope is manned by a safety officer whose job is to prevent the blindfolded 'skipper' from driving the submarine up the main street of Lamlash.

The skill of the navigator in plotting his EP is of paramount importance. It even ranks ahead of his local knowledge in identifying a headland like the Dodman or Anvil Point in a fleeting break of the visibility. Unhappily most yacht navigators do not know the difference between EP and DR.

Going offshore, the most important moment is to be able to lock the plot on to a reliable departure fix. Ideally this should be a tight set of three bearings on visual shore features. But a carefully-taken bearing on a dipping light is better than nothing, using the light's stated range as accurate to ± 1 mile at the moment when it drops down to being just a loom on the horizon. The precise cut-off moment can be determined by standing up in the cockpit and seeing the full light, while sitting down it is only a loom. Obviously this only applies in good visibility. Don't despair: I have taken simultaneous bearings on the looms of Start Point and the Casquets 70 miles apart.

In making an EP plot it is necessary to lay off all the factors which will cause the boat to deviate from her ordered course.

Much has been written about velocity triangles, but it is really very simple: plot the course and distance planned over a given time, then lay off the resultant of all the factors which will push the boat off that track, join them up and read off the course and speed made good (see p. 63). How to allow for leeway is a matter of judgement and experience of the boat. In a powerboat it is not a factor to be reckoned with. To judge the leeway being made by a sailboat, a rough indication can be found by looking over the transom at the wake. If it grows out to weather by 5° or more it is a clear warning that the boat is sliding to leeward by that amount while on the wind. Running or broad-reaching the leeway is negligible, but the navigator's problem is to know how much to lay off when the course is on the wind.

Here I must disagree with some of the pundits, who recommend allowing 2–3° leeway while on the wind, depending on its strength. But the fact is that the harder it blows the more the helmsman tends to luff up, thus making his own correction for leeway. However, a boat with a shallow canoe body like *Perseverance*'s 27in will slide off to leeward at an alarming rate, even with her centreboard down. The practical figure for her was not less than 10° leeway.

A powerboat with a high profile will be susceptible to leeway in a beam wind, but it is probably within the accuracy of the helmsman's course made good.

Plotting in practice

Starting from your departure from any well-known feature such as the Bembridge Ledge buoy, the Chichester Bar buoy, Portland Bill light or Berry Head, lay off the ordered course in degrees True, with the ship's time and log reading alongside its beginning: 0925 (22.7) means the fix was taken at 0925, when the log read 22.7. I always put the log reading in brackets so as to avoid any confusion with the time. Always assume you are about to run into impenetrable fog.

At 1000 it is time to settle into the routine of reading the log and marking up the EP on the chart. It now shows the log reading 25.9, in which case your DR position has advanced 3.2 miles along the plotted course. So measure 3.2 miles off the latitude scale and mark the new point on the course with 1000 (25.9).

If at the same time you get a reliable fix by shore bearings which puts you elsewhere, mark the chart 1000 (25.9)FIX. The discrepancy may be due to log error or tidal effect, but it is your most up-to-date certain position and should immediately be accorded the respect of a datum.

Never rub out chartwork until you are quite sure you have no further use for it. You may want to check back to clear up some doubts, for example to find out when or where the log (or more likely one of the electronic robots) started giving false readings.

A Fix is not something you get from Boots at Marble Arch just after midnight with a fresh prescription, but is just as morale-boosting, without being addictive. It means any position for your boat on the chart which can be relied upon with certainty. Using a hand-bearing compass this will involve taking 3 or more bearings at least 30° apart from each other. Once they have been converted to True bearings and laid off on the chart, with luck they'll cut in on top of each other, in which case you have a Fix, thus:

0900 (71.8) FIX

But if the plotted bearings do not fall so obligingly, you end up with a 'cocked hat'. If the area enclosed is small, take its mid-point as your Fix. If however it is large, you should treat it with caution and always assume your position to be on the edge of the cocked hat nearest any off-lying danger:

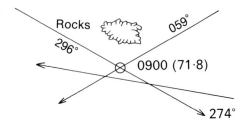

It could be the moment to take another set of bearings.

The most reliable visual bearing of them all is a transit, obtained by bringing two identifiable and charted shore features into line with one another. A classic one in daily use is that marking the Swashway channel leading from Spithead towards the beach at Southsea with a least depth of 2mo. By bringing into line the tall white Naval War Memorial on the front with the prominent spire of St Jude's church there is an unambiguous approach course on 048°T. The same technique applies to leading lights showing you the way into harbour. A transit is always designated as ∅ on a chart. Its great beauty is that the slightest deviation from it, whether due to cross tides or bad steering, is immediately apparent.

Experienced navigators accumulate a wealth of private transits, especially for racing round the buoys. The starting-line at Cowes sometimes has its outer limit mark 2.5 miles away, with one's view of the determining transit on the Royal Yacht Squadron battlements blotted out by hundreds of competitors' sails just when you most need to know whether it is safe to go for it. The trick is to get right on the line long before it is cluttered up by other boats and, from the pulpit right for'ard, select a transit high up on the Island shore which will be visible above the press of sails. It may be the right-hand edge (→|) of the Gloster Court flats in line with an oak tree on the skyline in Northwood Park.

Do not use fairway buoys for transits, as they tend to shift position slightly with the ebb and flow of the tide. Temporary buoys, such as inflatables laid by the Race Committee, can safely be assumed never to be in their advertised position. Starts from committee boats also call for private transits.

A transit coupled with a vertical sextant angle of the seaward mark forming it constitutes a Fix of high reliability.

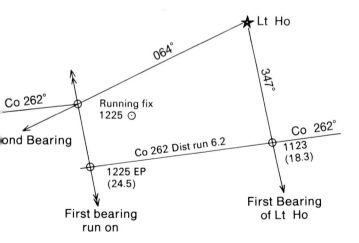

Plotting a running fix

A running Fix, much loved by instructors who make them look good on a blackboard, depends for its accuracy on knowing your precise course and distance over the ground between each bearing. But it may be better than nothing when only a single shore mark is in sight (e.g. the Eddystone Lighthouse when passing a long way to seaward or in poor visibility). The navigators take two consecutive bearings of the light at intervals giving no less than 30° change of bearing. After the first bearing has been laid off, the plot is run on to the point where the second one is taken. Then the first bearing is transferred forward by the distance run since it was taken. A parallel bearing line is drawn. Where it cuts the second bearing is the position of the Running Fix.

The accuracy of this method is totally dependent on the EP. In strong tides it can be considerably in error.

Station-pointer for 3-bearing fix

Horizontal sextant-angle or station-pointer fix measures the lateral angle between each of three prominent landmarks. By use of a special station-pointer with three adjustable arms you can then determine your exact position. Without a station-pointer you can reach the same result by drawing out the three bearings on tracing-paper and then slew it around until you set the only point where it fits all three shore marks. I reckon it to be rather an academic ploy and too fiddling for practical purposes in a small boat.

Station-pointer fix on three points 52° and 48° apart

Another trick is to make use of the fact that a right-angled isosceles triangle has the two sides enclosing its right-angle of identical length. So, take a bearing and note the time and log when a landmark is precisely 45° on the bow. The distance made over the ground until it comes abeam will also be the exact distance at which you are passing the mark to seaward.

A useful approximation for judging the distance by which you are going to pass outside a mark is to note its relative bearing, measured clockwise or anticlockwise from right ahead at a time when you have a reliable range, for example on raising a light. Provided you maintain course, the distance off when you get there will be;

$$\frac{\text{relative bearing in degrees}}{60} \times \text{the range}$$

Thus a light first spotted 24 miles off when 5° on the starboard bow will be left 2 miles when passing abeam. The sum is

$$\frac{\text{rel.bg } 5°}{60} \times 24$$

This mental aid holds good for relative bearings from right ahead to about 55° on the bow. It can also be used for judging the distance off track an oncoming ship will pass, assuming you are not closing on a collision course. Take the angle on the bow at which you observe the oncoming ship, divide it by 60 and multiply by the range for the amount of clear water there should be between you at your closest point . . . all things being equal.

Distance meter

Object 50ft half fills = 210 mins
Range in yards = 5.5 × 50
= 275 yards

300ft ship fills glass = 421 mins
Range in yards = 2.7 × 300
= 810 yards

when the object fills the field of view $R = 2.7 \times H$
if it half fills the field $R = 5.5 \times H$
if it occupies a quarter of the field $R = 11 \times H$
for simplicity, round it off to 3H, 6H and 11H, and you won't be far out.

There are special tables in the almanacs to give you the answer with greater accuracy, especially when using a sextant (see p. 104).

Range (or distance off) can be obtained by measuring the vertical angle of an object of known height. For this you can either use a sextant or an approximation based on finger-widths or the proportion of the field of view filled in your binoculars. Once you have the angle and the height, a useful mental aid for rangefinding is:

$$R \text{ (range in yards)} = \frac{H \text{ (height of object in feet)}}{A \text{ (vertical angle in minutes)}} \times 1150$$

It follows that whenever the height observed in feet is the same as the angle it subtends in minutes the range is 1,150yds. Thus a 100ft light measured at 1°40 is 1,150yds distant, while a 200ft tower at the same vertical angle is 2,300yds away (1.15nm), and so on.

Since the field of view of a pair of 7 × 50 binoculars subtends a fraction over 7° (421′),

DME held at arm's length

Distance Measuring Equipment (DME)
This is a card with a graduated frame cut in it. When held at arm's length an object of known height can be read off against a scale which in turn will give its range off an accompanying graph. There are other variations of this same principle on the market, but this one is obtainable from Wansbrough-White & Co, of Chiswick Mall, London W4 2PW.

Visual nav-aids There is nothing more reliable than a positively identified shore feature, whether it is a lighthouse, a church spire or an edge of land. But never ignore other sightings on which some reliance can be placed. The track of a cross-Channel ferry or a merchantman following the recommended course in a separation zone can be useful, as are the guard-ships on the Fastnet or the Plymouth-Roscoff ferry. If you get them right ahead or astern their course will be correct within 5°. The other certainty is to take a bearing when you are precisely abeam of them (the moment when the front of the bridge superstructure disappears) and then add or subtract 90°.

Commercial aircraft on flights to Deauville, Dinard or Le Touquet can also be useful. Sailing across the Atlantic on the trade wind route I found it comforting to have the boom-boom of the Concorde signalling its approach en route from Caracas to Dakar.

Other nav-aids Even if you have a constant lat-long read-out from Decca, Loran-C or Sat-Nav, don't count on any of them. In the 1983 Fastnet I navigated Arthur Emil's beautiful 51ft Petersen-designed *Artemis*. She was equipped with every known hi-tech nav-aid. Running down from the Fastnet to the Scillies we found ourselves in thick fog. With the wind from the WNW the fog-horn on the Bishop Rock was inaudible until we were almost on top of it. If we had relied on any of our electronic nav-aids we should certainly have driven on to the rocks not far from where Sir Cloudsley Shovell met his end.

On that occasion our EP was based on a fix obtained by the echo-sounder picking up the Labadie Bank cutting in with a good D/F bearing on Round Island on the north side of the Scillies. The tidal effect was negligible, so we hit off our desired landfall one mile south of the Bishop with no problem.

Later I patented an audio-nav tape which was intended to talk skippers into unfamiliar ports. An old submarine friend of mine, Peter Lucy, devised the circuitry necessary for the tape to be switched on and off at appropriate times, like 150 yards short of each mark upon which a new course had to be shaped. This depended on an input giving course and speed over the ground with some accuracy. After 2 years hawking the idea around the various manufacturers of electronic nav-aids we had to accept the fact that no one could produce the required degree of accuracy at a price which yachtsmen would be prepared to pay – if at all.

Radio direction-finding (D/F) also needs to be used with caution (see p. 77).

Tidal currents Only the Swiss, the PLO and Aztecs sail in waters without any tidal effect. So the strength and direction of the current must be built into any EP. The popular idea that the ebb and flood tides in the Channel cancel each other out on a 12-hour crossing to Cherbourg is a comforting notion, but not one that works in practice. For one thing it depends on your speed of advance (SOA), which might be 4kts at the start of the passage, slowly building to 7kts. The wisest move is to lay off your planned course on the chart, marking off where you hope to be each hour. Then take the aggregate tidal effect and run it off from the end of your plot as though you had sailed the boat in that direction. A line joining the start point and the end of the tidal offset will be what you should actually achieve.

Most tidal atlases give the strength of the tide at Springs and Neaps, so you must interpolate according to the state of the moon or the range of the tide. Whether reading off from the tidal information table on a chart or from a special tidal atlas the net result should be the same. Thus the mid-Channel ebb at Neaps might read as follows:

HW Dover	1hr after	250°	0.5
	2hrs after	250°	1.0
	3hrs after	245°	1.5
	4hrs after	245°	1.5
	5hrs after	250°	1.0
	6hrs after	250°	0.5

By inspection the total tidal effect over six hours is 6nm 248°. Assuming our own SOA through the water at 5.5kts on course 175° we now plot 33nm on 175° then transpose it 248° 6nm, giving course and speed made good 183° for 35nm (5.83 kts).

1800
(28.7)

Co 103°

sp 5.6kts

+ 1915 (35.7)

Co inc 3° windage and leeway – 106°

Co – made good 118° sp – 8 kts

Tide 3.6 – 155°

Dist. logged 1800–1915 = 7.0
On DR plot = 5.6 kts
On EP after allowing for 3kt
  tide and leeway = 8.0kts

1915 (35.7)

Plotting an EP

When your SOA is not consistently on 5.5kts, for example in a flat spot, the sums have to be reworked. This is one of the navigator's preoccupations when trying to lay off a course to hit a buoy like CH 1, where the tide runs strongly across the lay-line.

In developing a plot of your voyage it is necessary to mark the EP against the log-reading and time on the chart once an hour, on top of any intervening fixes which might present themselves. The latter may be passing close to an identifiable buoy or crossing a transit (two shore features falling into line) at a known distance offshore. This can be determined by cross-bearings or by measuring the height of the nearest object with a sextant. The Royal Navy used to have small monocular station-keepers which gave the range in cables of an object of known height by bringing the reflected image down to the bottom of the directly observed view of the object. I picked up my last one for £2, complete with polished mahogany case. They are now available in crummy plywood boxes for £650. A sextant does the same job, but is a bit clumsy to wield. Nautical almanacs all include tables for converting the observed sextant altitude for a known height into a distance. While racing this is the best method of determining whether you are gaining or losing on a competitor during a downwind leg (see p. 60).

The OPC is a constant source of anxiety to the navigator. It stands for Other People's Chartwork and can include such gems perpetrated by the Watch on deck as the longitude scale having been used for laying off distances, ignoring the decimal point on a digital log presentation or plotting a magnetic course without allowing for deviation or variation.

The correct scale for measuring distances on a Mercator projection (which includes nearly all charts in common use) is from the latitude appropriate to the waters in which you are sailing. Thus, to lay off 5.6nm on the plot, open the dividers to that distance as shown on the vertical side of the chart opposite the latitude you are on at the time.

A common source of egg on the navigator's face emerges when he transfers a plot from one chart to the other without the benefit of a recent fix. On a long offshore voyage always check back to see that the distance plotted bears close relation to your assumed SOA. It is surprisingly easy to gain or lose ten miles in the process.

Log errors At the end of a passage always compare your recorded log distance with that which you have actually sailed over the ground, especially on long reaching or running courses. If the comparison doesn't hold good after applying the net tidal effect, you may be tempted to adjust the log. Usually this is done in percentage terms by a clicker screw in the back of the console, but first check with the maker's manual (it should be in your Ship's Book). With a towed log you vary the pitch of the vanes according to a scale provided. My experience has been that one tends to over-react on suspected log errors. If you believe that the log is under-reading by 10%, try an adjustment of 5%. Most logs are very accurate, provided they have been installed or streamed in accordance with the maker's instructions.

Compass errors The likelihood that the master steering compass will develop a significant error during a voyage is hardly worth considering. To be on the safe side, check the sun's azimuth (i.e. true bearing) on rising or setting (see p. 21). The greatest source of course error can be attributable to the helmsman's simply not knowing what course he has averaged when called for a log entry. This often happens while racing, when a skilful light-weather helmsman may well sail on the boat-speed presentation, without even noticing what course he is steering.

Going for speed downwind

On a downwind leg even while cruising it pays to reach off, thus increasing apparent wind speed and boat speed. Sherman Hoyt taught Tom Sopwith a painful lesson on this subject by broad-reaching around *Endeavour* on a dead downwind leg when the Brits were heading for a 3-0 lead in the 1934 challenge for the America's Cup.

Controversy between the cockpit and the nav-station often surrounds the amount which can be profitably steered off the rhumb-line course. The figures are interesting and not generally understood. They are shown graphically on the opposite page:

Up to 25° off course you only need to find another 10% of boat speed to be gaining ground towards your objective against a boat which stays on the rhumb-line.

At 30° off it becomes 15%, so that boat speed has to go up from 6kts to 7kts to pay off. Thereafter it gets increasingly unattractive.

40° off is 23% below rhumb-line speed, so that you have to get $7\frac{1}{2}$kts to keep pace with a 6kt boat on the rhumb-line.

At 50° off you need to find 36% speed increase, or $8\frac{1}{4}$kts to hold your original 6kt SOA.

As the course deviation increases into left or right field you need to bear in mind how far you are getting away from your objective.

Navigating high-performance Offshore Powerboats

In a high-performance powerboat making over 40 knots offshore there is always the worry that the compass will not settle, with each slam into a head sea spinning like a roulette wheel. So I devised a sun compass, lifting the idea from the Long Range Desert Group's jeeps in World War II. This was no more than a sundial set forward of the driver's windshield

DEGREES OFF COURSE WHILE TACKING DOWNWIND

HOW FAR CAN YOU AFFORD TO REACH OFF DOWNWIND
Over 35° off-course starts to hurt

Speeds to make good in order to break even
(Percentage increase indicated)

SPEED OF ADVANCE (kts)	5%	10%	15%	20%	25%	30%	35%
4	4.2	4.4	4.6	4.8	5.0	5.2	5.4
5	5.25	5.5	5.75	6.0	6.25	6.5	6.75
6	6.3	6.6	6.9	7.2	7.6	7.8	8.0
7	7.35	7.7	8.05	8.4	8.75	9.1	9.45
8	8.4	8.8	9.2	9.6	10.0	10.4	10.8
9	9.45	9.9	10.35	10.8	11.25	11.7	12.15
10	10.5	11.0	11.5	12.0	12.5	13.0	13.5

ON THE RHUMB-LINE

with an azimuth ring adjusted for the anticipated time of our being halfway across Lyme Bar with 20 miles to go to the Skerries buoy south of the entrance to the River Dart. It worked beautifully.

Navigating a powerboat offshore, especially racing, calls for a technique of its own. Any idea that you can use a chart, dividers or a protractor is farcical. My solution was to have a tabulated flight plan giving the courses and distances between each mark on the course. These were presented as hours, minutes and seconds elapsed at every speed liable to be used during the race, accompanied by special descriptions of the lead-in features ashore: high rise apartment building at Boscombe, TV masts at Slapton, the right-hand edge of the trees near Christchurch when running in from the sou'west to pick up the North Channel buoy, and so on. Below are some extracts from the 1970 flight plan.

The same waterproofed card gave the extra speeds necessary to break even with our SOA if it was necessary to deviate from the straight course in order to get easier riding conditions on the long run across Lyme Bay. This idea first came to me when I was taking a Bertram 38 from Newhaven to Cowes. It was thick fog, visibility about 50 yards. Running with two turbo-charged Caterpillar diesels there was no chance of hearing a foghorn. So I timed a run from Newhaven to a point 2 miles downwind of the Owers light-vessel. When the stopwatch said we had run off the distance, I cut the motors. It was magic: there was the fog signal booming its head off right in front of us. Next thing we nearly hit the light-vessel. This technique also has its application to sailboats motoring in fog without the benefit of radar or any other form of reliable electronic nav-aid.

The higher your speed under power the more prudent it is to stop and take stock of any doubtful situation before proceeding. Last summer I was a guest in a 16kt powerboat heading for Cherbourg with less than total confidence in the compass. The visibility was less than a mile when a lighthouse suddenly appeared out of the spray and rain. Its light was not on, and it was too quickly identified as Cap de la Hague. Instead of killing the motor and getting a D/F check, we cheerfully headed east through what later turned out to be hazardous waters strewn with rocks. It soon became apparent that we had altered on sighting Cap Levi and had to retrace our steps gingerly to the westward.

Stage	Dist nm	Speed in knots						
		25	$27\frac{1}{2}$	30	$32\frac{1}{2}$	35	$37\frac{1}{2}$	40
		Times in hrs and mins						
Start–Sconce buoy	25.8	1.02	57	$51\frac{1}{2}$	48	44	$41\frac{1}{2}$	39
N Channel–Branksome	13.0	31	$28\frac{1}{2}$	26	24	$22\frac{1}{2}$	21	$19\frac{1}{2}$
Portland–Skerries	44.4	1.47	1.37	1.28	1.22	1.16	1.11	$1.06\frac{1}{2}$
Torquay–Portland	41.0	$1.38\frac{1}{2}$	$1.29\frac{1}{2}$	1.22	$1.16\frac{1}{2}$	1.10	$1.05\frac{1}{2}$	$1.00\frac{1}{2}$
Portland–N Channel	35.4	1.25	1.15	1.11	1.05	1.01	$56\frac{1}{2}$	53
N Channel–Finish	12.5	30	$27\frac{1}{2}$	25	22	$21\frac{1}{2}$	20	$18\frac{1}{2}$

Fog

Another situation which calls for more than straightforward DR plotting is finding one's way around in thick fog without the benefit of radar or reliable hyperbolic aids. Then the navigator soon reveals whether he possesses the two qualities sought by Napoleon in selecting a Marshal – he's not only got to be good; he's got to be lucky as well.

He has available to him only those nav-aids which are unaffected by zero-visibility conditions. More than ever it is necessary to know precisely what credence to place on the log, compass and echo-sounder. The latter can play a key role if the topography of the sea-bed has distinctive features, such as when crossing a clearly-defined depth contour. In certain circumstances it can add to your peace of mind if you stay in depths which would put a super-tanker hard aground.

A big tanker or container ship making 18 knots will keep on going straight ahead for nearly a mile before her ship's head starts to respond to an emergency wheel-order. She will come to rest up to 3 miles after Full Astern has been rung down. Even if the bridge watchkeepers spot you on their radar and she has sea-room in which to manoeuvre, there is no certainty that she will miss. In confined waters a new version of the right-of-way between sail and steam is enforced by local by-laws requiring yachts to keep clear at all times. My advice is to observe that rule even in a chance encounter in mid-Atlantic. The auto-pilot does not keep a look-out.

Such thoughts were uppermost in my mind soon after clearing the breakwater at Dunkerque in thick fog while delivering *Crusade* to Cowes. We were embarked along the narrow buoyed channel between the sandbanks and the French coast when thick fog descended. We felt our way buoy-hopping to the seaward end of the fairway and then were faced with beating across the main shipping lanes to reach the English coast, like crossing Piccadilly in the rush-hour blindfolded.

Heavy sirens boomed all round. No two members of the crew agreed about their bearings, as is often the case in fog. So we made for Cap Gris Nez 30 miles away, staying inside the 5-fathom line, going about the moment the echo-sounder said we could be sailing in waters with ships drawing 30 feet. That limited our liability to being run down by a trawler or a ferry. One of them passed close enough ahead for her wash to slop into our cockpit, but we didn't get a glimpse of her. Happily the fog lifted soon afterwards and we resumed our rhumb-line course.

The range at which radar will detect an echo is governed by the height of its antenna and the height of the target. It is near enough line-of-sight propagation. If you want to go bananas in a hurry, invest in a radar intercept receiver, which will pick up a transmission while it is too weak to make the return journey to its own antenna. These are much favoured by motorists with two strikes against them for speeding, always assuming they are on the same frequency as the police radar trap.

Their use at sea is limited by the fact that there are several radar frequencies in use, whereas commercial intercept gear will probably be limited to one of them. Even so, in crowded waters you'll be constantly on Red Alert.

Even in less frequented waters, the art of feeling one's way from one buoy to the next can go sadly awry if your chart shows only the major buoys. This is often the case with US and Canadian charts. Making our way to St Peters at the entrance to the Bras d'Or lakes we pressed on in thick fog in order to make a rendezvous in the locks. Confronted with having to negotiate the last few miles around the rocks in the Grand Grieve, our chart showed no buoys or beacons, so gave no indication whether to go round them clockwise, or the other way. We guessed wrong and found ourselves hard aground short of Jerome Point. The other channel was well marked but only on a large-scale chart, which we did not carry.

Fog Signals – fewer and quieter

Most lighthouse authorities have recognized that improved nav-aids and complaints from environmentalists point the way to cutting back on the number and audibility of fog signals. Trinity House, which looks after these matters in British waters, is committed to a policy of replacing all the big boomers powered by compressed air with nautophones. They have a 'usual range of 2 miles' which often means a lot less. It is much the same argument as seems to have won the day over VHF lighthouses (see p. 78). Unless yachtsmen are prepared to pay for their ongoing maintenance.

Many production boats are delivered ex-works with the steering compass as the only nav-aid installed. Within months some proud owners have equipped them with every known aid to navigation from radar to auto-steering – and then leave their boats alongside a marina for over 300 days a year.

At the outset, you alone can decide what you need beyond the Bare Necessities of Chapter 1. This in turn will depend on where and how you plan to sail – and what you are prepared to spend. If your ambition does not extend beyond local cruising in coastal waters, there is little point in going for Sat-Nav. Likewise radar need not be considered if your boat is too small to carry the antenna or scanner (typically 25in dia weighing 24lb, but in some sets up to 3ft dia and 40lb weight) securely mounted at a reasonable height above the water, preferably not less than 12ft. Or you may be going for flat-out racing and do not want the penalty of windage or weight aloft. Loran-C is not for you if you are going to be outside its coverage (see p. 72). Decca covers most of the Atlantic coast of Europe and the British Isles and the eastern seaboard of Canada north of Halifax.

The RORC's 1985 decision to lift all restrictions on hyperbolic and transmitting electronic aids has coincided with a proliferation of makes and types of equipment on the market. Clearly it is not sensible to rely solely on a salesman offering only his own products. Whereas most chandleries stock a fair selection of nav-aids and probably have all the brochures, few of them have staff who are qualified to give you all the pros and cons.

So ask around for a firm or a consultant who deals in all makes of equipment and can install whatever you choose. Each major yachting centre has this facility available, many with demonstration sets close at hand. You pay no more than list price and can negotiate a fixed cost for installation, knowing that it will be done expertly, avoiding such pitfalls as electronic or magnetic interference with other sets. Some offer interest-free 12 months' credit terms.

In 1985 the average cost of fitting new boats of all sizes delivered to the Hamble with the nav-aids selected by their owners was £1,200 for the smaller cruising boats and £8,000 for race-boats. So it is worth getting what you want. Some of the top IOR flyers add £30,000 to their price before the navigator feels he is properly supported.

Radar or Decca?
With radars starting at £1,300, hyperbolic aids or Sat-Nav around £1,000 without repeaters, many owners will have to start by deciding which one they can afford. The following table of comparisons between typical yacht radars and position fixing systems may help:

Characteristics	Radar	Position-finding device (Decca or Loran-C)
What the navigator sees	Continuous trace of coastline and all ships and other targets in range	No visual plan display. No data other than own ship
Presentation	Cathode ray tube with own ship in centre and concentric ranging rings on $\frac{1}{2}$–8m scales. Ship's head marker with relative bearings of all targets	Digital read-out of lat-long and hyperbolic lines on special lattice charts. Digital read-out of course being steered, or made good between fixes
Practical accuracy	$\pm 1°$ bearing. $\pm 15°$ vertical beam width. ± 50yds range (strobing error)	± 0.1 miles (200yds) in summer, often better. ± 0.2 miles in winter. Affected by proximity to land (e.g. in estuaries) and some propagation anomalies
Bad weather	Sea clutter masking small targets out to 1m. Heavy rain has local blanketing effect	Unaffected
Range	Approx line-of-sight subject to power output. Radar horizons = $1.22 \times \sqrt{\text{Antenna}+}$ target heights (ft) e.g. Antenna 16ft should pick up 60ft Lt Ho at $10\frac{1}{2}$nm	Within 250nm of master station for Decca, 1,000nm for Loran-C
Weight and Sizes:		
Antenna	25–40lb 25–30in dia	$1\frac{1}{4}$lb 3ft whip
Display/console	20–25lb 10in sq or up to 15in deep	$2\frac{1}{2}$lb 10in × 5in × $2\frac{1}{2}$in deep
Power (12V)	6.5 amps	0.2 amps
Watch out for:	Siting scanner within 4ft of compass; people with heart pacemakers are at risk	Vulnerability of antenna to rigging or sails

All systems offer continuous solutions so long as power does not fall below acceptable limits.

For the weekend cruising yachtsman forced to make a choice there is no doubt that the advantage lies heavily with radar. The navigator's problem is limited to bringing the boat within radar range of his intended landfall. It is important that the antenna be properly mounted. This is a big proviso, pretty well excluding all sailing boats under 25ft unless they are ketch of yawl rigged and have a mizzen mast for mounting the scanner.

There is a portable hand-held radar which plugs into the ship's 12V system or operates from its own battery. It is usually worn on a sling around the neck of someone on the foredeck. The antenna is incorporated and fixed, so bearing sense is obtained by swinging the set to pick up the echo on a narrow horizontal beam, in the manner of radio D/F. Its practical use is confined to picking up buoys fitted with radar reflectors at a range of $1\frac{1}{2}$–2 miles, depending on the sea-state. In the 1985 Halifax–St John Race there was visibility of less than a cable all the way from the start to the finish 240 miles away, but the Whistler, as we called it, managed to pick up the critical buoys which were turning-marks off Cape Sable. We stormed over the finish line under spinnaker without even seeing the committee boat, but they had us on their radar and, once again, the Whistler obliged. Commercially the set is now known as 'Ranger Radar'.

Radar Beacons (*Racon*)   Certain lighthouses and buoys are fitted with transponders which pick up an extraneous radar transmission and fire it back so that it appears as a rectangular slug on the transmitting ship's PPI display. In some cases it may have a coded identification (e.g. the Seven Stones LV, which the *Torrey Canyon* failed to notice, emits a letter 'O' ---at the tail end of its trace). Racon beacons are designated 'Racon' on Admiralty charts. Their particulars can be found in any nautical almanac.

Depending on antenna height, Racon beacons should be picked up at 10 miles.

Radar reflectors   The echo returned by a small GRP boat is unremarkable and easily lost in rough seas. To enhance the echo in poor visibility you should hoist a radar reflector as high as you conveniently can. There are two types:

(a) A diamond-shaped structure made of three flat interlocking aluminium sheets between 12″ and 20″ square. The advantage claimed for this type is that it can be dismantled and stowed away flat in a canvas pouch. But strong men have been driven to drink when it comes to reassembling it and getting all its corners securely locked into a rigid structure. Experience of putting together oriental wooden puzzles helps.

(b) A GRP cylinder about 2ft long and 9in in diameter filled with aluminium foil has a nominal echoing area of 9sq ft, which is a substantial improvement on the biscuit-tin model described above. They look neater and can be more easily secured so as not to flap around while hoisted, but at about £60 they cost 3–4 times more than the diamond puzzle does.

An even better solution would be a 3cm waveband transponder which amplifies the signal from the detecting radar and throws it back with interest. At one time it was proposed that the RORC should make these available for yachts racing across the steamship lanes in the English Channel, but it was decided that 150 beefed-up lozenges all painted simultaneously on the radar receiver of a merchantman would create too much confusion.

Or perhaps sparmakers will oblige by building radar echo-enhancers into the rig.

Sat-Nav

Existing satellite navigation receivers in yachts rely on the US Navy's Transit system, 6 satellites which have been in polar orbit since 1964 and are no longer evenly spaced. There are certain limitations:

(a) An initial DR accurate to ±6onm has to be fed in, and then a warm-up period of 15 minutes is necessary. The receiver digests the signals from the satellite during each pass lasting about 15 minutes. It measures the doppler shift (high frequency on approach, low going away), notes its closest point of approach and is automatically told enough by the satellite's message to work out an instant fix for the boat.

(b) Satellites passing below 20° or over 70° latitude are unreliable and will be rejected by the receiver.

(c) The interval between fixes is 1–1½ hours, depending on one's own latitude. If one or more satellites has an off-day, the fixing interval can stretch to over 4 hours.

(d) A computer updates the lat-long position between fixes but is susceptible to errors of input, especially of speed made good over the ground. The practical accuracy for a stationary boat is ±400yds (0.2nm) provided all goes well. Each knot of error in own speed input will induce 0.2nm error.

The advantages for Sat-Nav are:

(a) It is the best available alternative to Decca or Loran-C outside their coverage area, especially if astro-nav is not available.

(b) The antenna is small (12in × 7in), non-rotating and weighs just over 2lb. It can be located anywhere above decks.

(c) Its power consumption is low, using 12–36 volts at 20W. Some sets have an internal battery giving 15 minutes' back-up life in the event of a ship's power failure.

The Transit system will be in service at least until 1994.

Decca This British hyperbolic navigation aid gives continuous fixing within its area of coverage – 250 miles of the Atlantic coast from the North Cape to the SE coast of Spain and also off NE Canada. All being well it will deliver its claimed accuracy of one cable at 100nm. Latitude and longitude are shown by digital presentation. It needs a verifying departure fix to get its act together quickly. It can coach the helmsman to pre-set lat/long positions known as way-points.

Loran-C
The well-proven Long Range Aid to Navigation (Loran-C) covers within 1,000nm of the coast of the USA, the Mediterranean from the eastern coast of Spain to Cyprus and the waters of the British Isles and Norway to the north and west of a line joining the Fastnet Rock and the Skaggerak. Its position accuracy is generally ±0.3nm but has its lapses in certain areas of poor propagation. It operates on 100kHz and measures the Time Difference (TD) between signals from a master station arriving at two or more slave stations. These are plotted on special lattice charts giving the hyperbolic lines of TDs in micro-seconds. Coverage may be extended to the whole of the British Isles and its approaches, in which case it may be a candidate to replace Decca for yachts.

All modern sets translate this data to lat-long digital displays, *but*:

Always do an occasional check of the lat-long displayed on the receiver against a plotted fix of TDs on a Loran-C chart, because it may sometimes be more accurate than the microprocessor solution. Another reason for not relying solely on the lat-long display is that there may be times when one set of TDs is out of kilter and showing amber or even red warning lights on the receiver, while the other is still reliable.

In 1985 I was navigating *Toscana* from St John, New Brunswick, to Mount Desert Island near Bar Harbor, Maine, normally an easy trip of 125 miles along one of the most beautiful coast lines in the world. But the visibility was less than a cable, the wind was 20 knots on the nose and I had a flight to catch. Soon after sailing our Loran-C receiver served notice that it was no longer prepared to help.

Our progress motor-sailing through the narrow rock-bound

straits between Grand Manan Island and the Canadian border had to be hand-plotted from one whistle buoy to the next, often having to cut the engine to pick up the sound of each buoy, then creep up to it for positive identification.

Ten miles short of Mount Desert we broke out into sunshine and maximum visibility. My sleepless night could have been made less anxious if I had spotted soon enough that one of the Loran-C TD-lines ran straight through the Grand Manan Straits to our destination and that it had performed faultlessly although its 'pair' was unable to produce any kind of a lat-long fix.

However, Mount Desert Island is shown in *Eldridge's Pilot Book* as an area in which Loran-C is liable to local propagation errors of up to 1,300 yards, so you can't win them all.

Loran-C is to all intents and purposes as accurate as Decca in its own waters. American microchip and computer technology have led the way with dozens of different makes of receivers, each neater, simpler to operate and sometimes cheaper than last year's model. It always needs a whip antenna of its own, generally fitted to the taffrail.

The Global Positioning System (GPS) GPS has seven satellites in orbit already, mostly in military use, but only providing about 6-hours' coverage a day, although US manufacturers selling the system to yachtsmen interfaced with (i.e. linked to) Loran claim 'up to 18 hours' in the northern hemisphere. The full GPS system giving 24-hour worldwide instant fixes will require 18 satellites up there, plus 3 spares parked in orbit all designed to be launched from the cargo bay of a space shuttle. Hence the delay of GPS coming into service, now admitted to be 1991 or later.

It does not work on doppler measurement but on timing the difference between several satellites' transmissions and their reception on board. For civilian users including yachtsmen its accuracy will be ± 100 yards, deliberately degraded to prevent hostile nations' enjoying the ± 15 yards planned for the military. Initially the sets look like costing as much as a Half-Tonner, but no doubt the Japanese will have other ideas.

OMEGA Until GPS becomes a reality and within reach of a weekend yachtsman's budget, there is only one worldwide continuously-available position fixing system. Here I discount celestial navigation, for it is surprising how far you can sail without seeing the sun or getting stars under conditions suitable for hacking them down.

In 1960 I was dismasted in the Transatlantic Race in *Drumbeat*. We made it to St John's, Newfoundland, where her old spare wooden mast duly arrived on a Bowater newsprint ship from London. The subsequent crossing to Brixham took a little under 11 days. We sailed through the iceberg belt in thick fog and then ran before a succession of warm fronts the whole way over, without ever seeing the sun or the stars. Our landfall was verified by echo-sounder and radio D/F bearings on Round Island, at the northern end of the Scillies.

The system which might have helped under such circumstances is Omega developed by the US Navy around the same time the US Coast Guard was perfecting Loran-C. It has worldwide accuracy of ± 2nm by day, but possibly twice as much by night. It transmits on VLF (10–14Kc, or kHz nowadays) not far off the frequencies used to communicate with submerged submarines. The master stations all require antennae of up to 2 miles in length, usually slung between adjacent mountain peaks, as they are in Norway, Alaska, the Rockies, Australia, Japan, Argentina, Liberia and Reunion Island.

Unlike submarines, yachts can receive these signals on a whip antenna only 7ft long and which are digested in a box no bigger than a Loran-C or Decca console.

Various propagation anomalies have to be allowed for and

special US lattice charts used for plotting. However, all these difficulties can be overcome by having a Differential Omega receiver which takes in rebroadcast laundered position lines accurate to within $\frac{1}{4}$ mile when you happen to be within 50 miles of one of the monitoring stations. Unhappily these are far between; for example, from Dover to Gibraltar is 1,250 miles, but the monitoring rebroadcast stations along the route (Cap Gris Nez opposite Dover, Ushant, Cap Finisterre at the NW tip of Spain and Lagos just east of Cap St Vincent) only cover 350 miles of the route. A modern receiver will come up with lat-long.

For around £5,000 you can get a Tracor so-called Global Navigation System which links Omega to Sat-Nav and keeps a continuously updated position on display.

On balance Omega does not rate high on the weekend navigator's shopping list.

Integrated systems
(Only rich owners of cruising boats need read this section, unless they are liable to be invited to race in an IOR boat and want some understanding of the cross-talk between helmsman, navigator and sail trimmers).

Long before the RORC allowed computer-aided systems to take the inputs from any sensors (e.g. wind direction and speed from the masthead, speed and distance run from an underwater log, course from a transmitting magnetic compass and depth from an echo-sounder) and display a wide option of tactical solutions, Brookes & Gatehouse offered its first Hercules system. This was accompanied by a list of functions which were on offer and a warning of those forbidden during RORC races. Some, such as calculating True Wind Speed and Direction or Vmg (the speed made good along the rhumbline), could be simply arrived at by manual plotting, using elementary velocity triangles. Meanwhile Hercules was doing

it all for you, at the touch of a button, but the navigator was not supposed to peek unless the boat was flying its ensign, and thus not under the rules of racing.

Brookes & Gatehouse were mainly using analogue displays (clock-face) but, along with their ever-growing range of competitors, increasingly now offer alternative digital displays. Currently their super Hercules 390 system for a raceboat will cost over £5,000 plus installation charges. Nowadays there are no restrictions against using the whole system during races.

Many of the functions on offer seem to be there more to demonstrate the versatility of the system than to answer any long-felt need. True enough single-handed sailors can gain comfort from having alarm hooters sound off on any major change in wind direction or depth, but they have not prevented some spectacular shipwrecks, simply because, like commuters, sailors can sleep through alarm calls. Perhaps that may explain the disappearance of some singlehanded sailors.

Battery voltage, seawater temperature, heel angle and timing an egg to boil can now all be shown on digital displays simply by selecting the right channel.

Many instrument makers recognize that the wide spectrum of information shown simultaneously to the helmsman can be confusing even to the most experienced racing crews and amounts to an expensive overkill for a cruising boat – like fitting a 747 instrument panel in a Tiger Moth. So now simplified sailing monitors are available, which confine themselves to presenting the log, speed, wind and battery voltage displays. One such is the B & G Hornet.

It is as well to bear in mind the following factors which can distort the end-product of microprocessors and give the helmsman false guidance, mostly in very light winds:

(a) Even in a boat with a moderate mast-height there will be days when the wind speed and direction may be different on deck to those at the masthead whence your sensors are sending down their messages to the instruments over the chart-table. Some modern maxis have extra wind sensors fitted halfway up the mast, seeking to measure the average strength and direction of the wind which is powering the sail plan, rather than that which shows on the burgee or ensign.

As a schoolboy I recall being alone in a 9ft 6in Lymington Scow totally becalmed in the middle of the Solent when the entire J-Class fleet sailed through me at 6kts, propelled by a breeze which only existed 75ft above the surface. The bearded man at the wheel of *Britannia* had a familiar look and an unforgettable vocabulary, as he suggested I should get my bloody boat out of the xxxx way. The Americans refer to this phenomenon as 'wind sheer'. It has little relevance to cruising boats, most of which would have their kedges down or their motors on before the situation arises.

(b) Although carefully balanced and machined, there is some mechanical friction in masthead wind sensors, which can lead to erroneous inputs down below. There is also the effect of heavy rolling or lurching. These are especially apparent when the wind is from astern and the relative wind on the knife-edge of zero.

Nowadays it is hard to find someone who is available to light a cigarette and let the smoke tell where the zephyrs are coming from. I recommend a Chinese joss-stick on a wire stick which can be stuck on the cabin top and give off a steady, slow-burning smoke signal. After all the Captain of a big aircraft-carrier relies more on a smoke trace emitted along the flight deck near the axis of the catapult than from any instrument.

Some boat owners collect nav-aids like motorists do club car-badges, so I end this section with a word of advice to anyone putting total reliance in his instruments, if only because they cost him so much. Don't react too quickly to any change in circumstance or sailing efficiency being shown on the dials. Don't rush into changing sheet settings; let them settle for a minute or more before deciding that the new data has to be acted upon.

On the last Bermuda Race I coined a phrase for our trigger-happy helmsmen and sail trimmers: DDD (Digital Dial Dementia). The same people who are quite accustomed to applying the five-minute rule and making sure of the new breeze before initiating a sail change react as though they are ducking a mugger's knife when Polar Boat Speed – an esoteric efficiency measurement drawn up for an individual boat on different points of sailing – drops a tenth of a knot.

Recently I heard of a freak error induced by blind obedience to Decca. A Class I ocean-racer was leading the fleet, broad reaching on starboard on a black stormy night. When the skipper came on deck he noticed that the boat was now reaching off on the opposite tack, still making close to hull speed. 'That was a big wind shift', he commented.

Not so. The helmsman was steering by a digital compass dictated by Decca guiding them to the next way-point – an arbitrarily chosen tactical milestone, often the next mark on the course. He assumed they had overstood, and the black box was putting him right; or perhaps he thought they'd reached one way-point and were now on course to the next. Somehow he'd missed the buzzer which alerts the navigator to the end of one leg and the start of another.

A lat-long check on the chart showed that the boat had sailed nearly a reciprocal course for 3 miles, which ultimately cost them the race.

The reason was that someone had inadvertently hit the man-overboard button on the set, which was now faithfully conning the boat back to the exact position where the non-event had occurred.

It could just as easily happen with a Loran-C linked integrated system.

Radio Direction-finding (D/F)

Radio and Radar Chart Symbols

All Admiralty charts nowadays have a violet circle around the lighthouse or buoy carrying radio or radar aids. The letters alongside identify their functions, as follows:

Ro Bn	Radio beacon of any kind
RC	Non-directional radio beacon
RD	Directional radio beacon with its transmitting beam identified by a bearing: i.e. 221°30′ over a pecked line
RW	Rotating pattern radio beacon
RG	Radio Direction-finding station
R	Coast Guard station offering QTG service
Aero RC	Aeronautical radio beacon
Racon (K)	Radar transponder beacon on 3cm(X) band 'K' Morse identification
Racon (K) (10cm)	As above on S band (10cm)
Ramark	Radar beacon transmitting without being triggered off by a ship's radar.

Omni-directional marine radio beacons operating on long-wave frequencies between 275 and 315kHz have been used by yachts for over 50 years. The more powerful transmitters can usually be relied upon to give a single bearing to an accuracy of $\pm 5°$ out to a range of 50 miles by day. The commonest form of receiver is one with a ferrite rod aerial mounted across the axis of a hand-held magnetic compass. Once the station has been identified by frequency and call-sign (see nautical almanacs for this information) the D/F set is held as far away from the boat's magnetic influences as practicable, with the operator wearing a headset, rather than relying on loud-speakers against competing ambient noise. Most prefer a bat-tery-operated set with no trailing power leads. Around £150 will buy one with push-button tuning and a trigger lock to clamp the compass rose and read off the null without losing it on the next lurch of the boat.

The shore station might be St. Catherine's Lt. at the southern extremity of the Isle of Wight. It is listed as:

Call sign 'CP'	—.—. .——.
Frequency	291.9kHz
Range	50nm
Transmission sequence	2 mode A2A

The reliable range for getting good bearings is not more than 25 miles by night. Most marine radio beacons are on air for one minute ten times each hour. In the example above, the sequence No 2 tells you that 'CP' comes on at 01,07,13 … 55 minutes past each hour. It is preceded by Portland Bill ('PB') No. 1 and followed by Cap d'Antifer ('TI') No.3. After Antifer come Le Havre Lanby ('LH') No.4, Pte de Ver Lt in the middle of the D-Day beaches ('éR') is No.5 and Barfleur ('PG') No.6, before restarting the sequence with Portland Bill again.

Each transmission lasts exactly 60 seconds, starting with the call-sign repeated 4 times, then a steady note for 25 seconds and signing-off with the call-sign twice. Don't be confused by the A2A designation. It applies to all but a handful of marine radio beacons and means that the carrier wave (basic signal note) is switched on throughout, even when the note is modulated to give the call-sign and 25 seconds steady signal intended for taking a bearing. This facility is intended for commercial sets with automatic lock-on.

Having switched on and tuned to the precise frequency, be ready to use any one of various switching positions intended to filter out extraneous noise by use of the Beat Frequency Oscillator (BFO).

To take the bearing during the 25-second steady note, hold the antenna as nearly horizontal as possible and sweep it gently back and forth across the point where the null occurs. This is the moment when the transmitted signal drops to its lowest point, or even cuts out altogether. The more distinct the contrast between the null and the D/F signal and the smaller the arc through which it is observed, the more reliable the bearing thus obtained. In practice it is better to note the bearing to the left where the audio note starts to diminish, than read off its right-hand edge, when it comes on strongly again. Split the difference and you have your observed D/F bearing. The wider the null arc, the greater the likelihood of error.

There are however a few sleepers in this neat-sounding procedure. The first is the Quadrantal Error induced by the radio waves being bounced or reflected off the boat's rig and structure. They have the effect of bending the signal. They are at their most pronounced in a boat with metal frames, rigging and guardwires which have not been 'insulated' by having rope seizing at each end; the worst errors occur on either bow or quarter. Some D/F suppliers offer to swing the set against observed visual bearings of a D/F transmitter and fudge a 'deviation' card which looks good – as any smoothed-out sinusoidal curve should – but in practice is not much help, especially since most D/F bearings at sea are taken when the boat is heeled over.

Reaching in towards the end of the 1984 Bermuda Race I picked up Gibb's Hill and Kinley Field D/F stations loud and clear with a small, well-defined null. There was no question of getting a cut from them, as the bearings were less than 20° apart. But both confirmed a suspicion that there was an easterly set which had carried us too far off our desired rhumb-line for a racing landfall. Loran-C had been of dubious value since we had pounded our way through wind-against-current for several hundred miles and the whole set was in intensive care, with silicone spray trying to dry off the antenna junction box.

We were about to tack to the westward, when a single sun sight at right angles to our track showed that both our precise D/F bearings had been slewed 15° by quadrantal error.

Some of the 1985 Admiral's Cup boats were still using a remote D/F antenna mounted on a staff above the taffrail with a morse cable drive to rotate it. Heeling error is reduced by tilting the antenna housing by hand into approximately the horizontal plane.

D/F bearings are also affected when taken at a narrow angle to a high coast-line.

In spite of its drawbacks, radio D/F can be useful in rounding a headland on which its transmitter is sited.

Aero beacons have the advantage of transmitting continuously, but many are situated some distance inland with high ground intervening and introducing further errors.

Any kind of D/F bearing lends itself to being misread as a reciprocal bearing; but, except for transmitters situated in the open sea, such as the Casquets (west of Alderney) or les Roches Douvres (midway between Guernsey and the Brittany coast), the bearing 'sense' is generally self-evident, but keep it in mind.

Calibration By prior notice to the Lighthouse authority (Trinity House in Great Britain) you can arrange to get a transmission for calibration purposes within 5 miles of a few selected Rdo.Bn stations. They are listed in the almanacs, but I can't see the point in the rather formal procedure involved, when you can always pick off a shore station whilst on passage and check against visual bearings.

Details of Radio Aids The principal nautical almanacs and the *Admiralty List of Radio Signals*, Vol. 2 contain all the information you need.

Other Radio Aids If you have a VHF receiver there are

two additional radio aids which give a bearing accurate to ±2° unaffected by any of the yacht's own errors in taking D/F bearings out to 30 miles in good conditions.

(a) *VHF Direction-Finding Service* operated by 20 Coast-guard shore stations around the UK, each of which is shown on the chart with the symbol 'RG'. On a passage along the South Coast they are located at Pendennis at the entrance to Falmouth, Rame Head SW of Plymouth Sound, Berry Head at the western end of Torbay, Portland Bill, Stenbury Head near Ventnor in the Isle of Wight, Fairlight near Hastings and South Foreland, the most prominent white cliff of Dover. Lovers of the rollicking sea shanty 'Spanish Ladies' will now know where Fairlight is, mentioned in the Grand Fleet's progress up-Channel as the last headland before Dungeness. The full list can be found in nautical almanacs or the *Admiralty List of Radio Signals*, Vol. 2.

This is a service for use in emergencies, but not necessarily terminal ones. For example a boat lost near a lee shore in bad visibility without radar or radio D/F functioning could follow the drill.

Constant watch ashore is kept on Channel 16, the universal distress frequency (156.800mHz). If it is not a distress message the yacht should call on Channel 67 (156.375mHz, the universal Coastguard net). The shore station will call on the same frequency, giving the yacht's True bearing *from* the shore station.

There are also RG facilities on Guernsey at the airport $2\frac{3}{4}$ miles WSW of St Peter Port and Jersey near La Corbière Lt Ho at the SW extremity of the island. Both listen on Channel 16 and Guernsey has Channel 67 for its working frequency, but Jersey uses Channel 82 (161.735mHz).

If asked, certain Coastguard stations will put out a signal for the yacht to check its own D/F bearings. The service is known as QTG and its transmitter shown on charts with the letter R.

VHF Lighthouses

At present there are two VHF shore beacons putting out a continuous rotating directional signal on Channel 88 (162.025mHz) which will give a yacht ±2° accuracy of bearing in all conditions of weather, angle of heel or ship's head out to about 20 miles, without any worries about quadrantal error. The stations are on Anvil Point and Scratchells Bay by the Needles. Yachtsmen have found it invaluable making the Needles with a cross-bearing from Anvil Point, whose signal alternates every minute with Scratchells Bay.

Many other narrow channels could usefully be illuminated in this way (for example making St Peter Port breakwater from the Little Russel Channel; along the south coast of Jersey to St Helier; or the entrance to Poole Bay, Deauville or Plymouth Sound). But at the time of writing (1987) Trinity House are in some difficulty to find even the modest sum needed for annual maintenance – about the equivalent of campaigning a Half-Tonner for a season. It seems that commercial shipowners have no need of the service, and no one can see how to prise the money out of yachtsmen. So, far from extending the service, there is the possibility that the service will slowly lapse, although there may be second thoughts and new locations farther west.

Its operation is dead simple. After station identification in Morse code, start counting the beats until there is a sudden null. Then refer to the table and read off the bearing of the VHF lighthouse in degrees (True) from the yacht. The following table is for Anvil Point and Scratchells Bay. From it will be seen that a null at a count of 47 means the Scratchells Bay VHF lighthouse bears 057° True. In case you get lost counting the beats, there is a distinct change of tone after every ten.

	Count of Beats	0	1	2	3	4	5	6	7	8	9
V3 Anvil Point Lt Ho	0	–	–	–	–	–	–	–	247	249	251
Call-sign: AL (· − · − · ·)	10	253	255	257	259	261	263	265	267	269	271
Sector: 247°–007°	20	273	275	277	279	281	283	285	287	289	291
Range: 14 miles	30	293	295	297	299	301	303	305	307	309	311
Alternate with	40	313	315	317	319	321	323	325	327	329	331
Scratchells Bay (V6)	50	333	335	337	339	341	343	345	347	349	351
	60	353	355	357	359	001	003	005	007	–	–
V6 High Down Scratchells Bay	0	–	–	–	–	–	–	–	337	339	341
0.4m Needles Lt 280°	10	343	345	347	349	351	353	355	357	359	001
Call-sign: HD (· · · · − · ·)	20	003	005	007	009	011	013	015	017	019	021
Sector: 337°–097°	30	023	025	027	029	031	033	035	037	039	041
Range: 30 miles	40	043	045	047	049	051	053	055	057	059	061
Alternate with	50	063	065	067	069	071	073	075	077	079	081
Anvil Point Lt. (V3)	60	083	085	087	089	091	093	095	097	–	–

CONSOL Known as Consolan in the States, this is a wartime long-range passive radio aid, calling for no more than an MF receiver, a Consol chart (or tables giving bearing lines) and an ability to count up to 60 and determine when the dots stop and the dashes start. In practice there is usually a blurred null which is middled to get the bearing. Thus 32 dashes and 21 dots, leaves 7 unidentified. The answer is $35\frac{1}{2}$ dashes, $24\frac{1}{2}$ dots.

The range is certainly up to 1,000 miles, so it calls for the application of half-convergency tables to allow for the difference between Mercator and Great Circle plotting. It is unsuitable for coastal navigation or for making a landfall. Furthermore the system is now obsolescent and reduced to one transmitting station in Europe: Stavanger on 319kHz.

Forget it.

NAVTEX This is a simple telex receiver operating on a fixed MF frequency of 518kHz using 12V DC which receives a print-out of urgent navigation notices to mariners, gale warnings, twice daily shipping forecasts, search and rescue (SAR) alerts, nav-aid alerts when any of the position-finding systems develop problems. It is compact, about the size of *Reed's Almanac*, can be left on 'stand-by' using only a 2ma trickle of juice, going up to 2amps while printing incoming messages. A standard wire antenna is supplied with the basic set at about £500; a whip antenna for optimum reception will add another £100. Using the service is free.

The International Maritime Organisation is aiming for all ships to carry Navtex, with the intention that one day there will be worldwide coverage within 200 miles of any coast line.

At present there are transmitters at Niton on the Isle of Wight, Brest-le Conquet opposite Ushant and Ostend, between them covering the whole of the English Channel comfortably, with others in Scotland and the Baltic.

The information put out is geared to the needs of commercial shipping and is not too comprehensive on coastal or inshore data. However, it is said that a small ships' service may be started up. Until it does, it is low on any yachtsman's optional extras.

Needless to say the Japanese have entered the lists, offering a receiver printing out not only Navtex but weather facsimile synoptic charts (FAX).

Twenty years ago R/T was about as likely to be found in a weekend yachtman's boat as in the family mini. But, as with household appliances, TV sets and music systems, they have ridden the microchip revolution in a buyer's market.

Since the advent of Citizen's Band radio (CB) and cellular circuits you don't have to be head of Mogul Oil to keep in constant touch with the outside world. One enthusiast told me he had fitted a car telephone to avoid the frustration of pulling in at a coin-box and finding it out of order.

So it is with yachts. VHF radio-telephones are available for under £250. Within the limitations of their range (somewhat better than line-of-sight) and the number of channels with which they are equipped, they are very much on the increase. RYA figures show that in the four years since 1982 the number of UK-licensed R/T yacht operators has more than doubled – from 4,000 to 9,000. My guess is that the number of sets in use must be over 20,000 in British waters. It is now mandatory for many offshore races.

Apart from calling in from seaward to enquire about the next time the lockgates will open, to book a berth or to alert the Customs, R/T is as important for your own safety as it may be for others in distress. A fire at sea or sudden flooding may give you time to get off a distress call by voice, in the certain knowledge that all commercial ships will be keeping a loudspeaker watch on the distress frequency, Channel 16 (156.800 mHz) even if you are out of range of a shore station. It is also useful for getting weather forecasts from the coastguard.

Modern sets are light, compact, easily installed and no more difficult to operate than a TV set, unless you are tongue-tied or have not grasped the procedure (see p. 82). During the 1979 Fastnet Race only the 57 boats competing for the Admirals Cup had to carry VHF sets and report their positions regularly. The other 250 boats were required to carry only a signal light and distress flares for communicating with the outside world.

When the extent of the disaster which had struck the fleet became apparent, the BBC Radio News tacked on a message from the Race Committee asking that all yachts able to do so should report their positions. I switched on the VHF set, got an encouraging red light to show that it was powered up and identified ourselves to the outside world, with the ammeter flickering back and forth as I spoke. By this time there was a fleet of rescue craft and aircraft all talking on Channel 16, but no one answered. After repeatedly sending out an unacknowledged message, the skipper agreed to use his single side-band (SSB) HF transmitter, which had 8 times the power of the 25W VHF set, an independent antenna and a range of several thousand miles. It also cost 15 times as much.

Generally it is only permitted to be used at half-power during some races and not at all in others, except in an emergency. On this occasion we got straight through via Portishead. Later we noticed that our masthead VHF whip antenna had been blown away in the storm.

Regulations to be observed

The paperwork called for before you first switch on and put through a ship-shore call is daunting, but mostly a one-off exercise. The following licences must be carried by UK-based yachts.

(a)   The Ship licence at £17.50 allows one to transmit or receive. This licence will allocate the ship's call-sign, usually

4 letters. Incredibly a £12.50 annual fee is required just to receive transmissions from shore. Application should be made to the Home Office, Radio Regulatory Division, Waterloo Road, London SE1 8AU. Even a set intended only for emergency use needs a licence.

(b)   Evidence that the set conforms to technical standards also laid down by the Home Office. Most sets are sold with their type already approved.

(c)   A Certificate of Competency for the operator who will have control of the set. For most yachtsmen this means a Restricted Certificate (VHF only), obtainable from the examining authority, the Royal Yachting Association, Victoria Way, Woking, Surrey GU21 1EQ. For £1.50 they will send you RYA booklet G26 which gives the syllabus and how and where to offer yourself for examination – sometimes in your own boat. There is a one-off fee of £13. All the examiner sets out to do is assure himself that you know the voice procedures and how to work the set. For some inexplicable reason this Certificate is only open to British, Irish or Commonwealth citizens. Foreign nationals living in the UK and keeping a boat here must have been certificated by their own national authorities, although exceptions may be made on request.

(d)   A copy of Section 11 of the Post Office (Protection Act) which binds operators to respect the confidentiality of intercepted traffic. It comes with the Ship Licence.

(e)   A list of coastal radio stations likely to be used, with all their operating schedules.

(f)   A radio telephone log – this may be satisfied by making a note of any R/T working in the Deck Log.

(g)   A copy of Notices to Ship Wireless Stations, obtainable from British Telecom International, Maritime Division, 23 New Fetter Lane, London EC4 1AE.

Rules governing operating sets
(a)   Follow correct voice procedures (see below)
(b)   Absolute priority to be given to distress traffic
(c)   Do not transmit on top of another station
(d)   Respect confidentiality of intercepted traffic
(e)   No obscenity
(f)   Do not use distress channels for routine traffic although Channel 16 can be used for calling up another ship only, then switching to another assigned channel
(g)   All transmitted messages must identify the yacht concerned
(h)   Ship-to-ship R/T transmissions in harbour are forbidden, but ship-shore is permitted.

Procedures
(a)   First, make sure the channel selected is clear and then proceed, first naming the station being called and then give own identification. There are special calling frequencies listed for all shore stations. Do not call them on Ch 16. Now proceed:
'Niton Radio (this is) yacht *Lullubelle* – over.' 'Over' means you have switched off your transmitter and are listening for a reply. If you do not get an answer it pays to add 'Do you read me', which may bring in another station who could relay your message. When you have established contact, give your message clearly, where necessary repeating or even spelling phonetically words likely to be misread:
'Intend proceeding to join yacht *Nephele* ... I spell November Echo Papa Hotel Echo Lima Echo ... at Hamble Point marina berth C for Charlie Two at 1615 ... over.'

The receiving station will give either 'Roger' or 'Received' and, if he has nothing further to add, 'out' denoting end of conversation. If the message has not been received or understood, he should ask 'say again' or 'say again after Hamble Point ... over.'

If in doubt, have the phonetic alphabet from Alfa to Zulu showing near your set with the phonetic numerals from Won to Zero.

(b) *Distress and emergencies on Channel 16:*

At any time of grave danger, go straight on the air with 'Mayday' three times followed by 'this is *Lulubelle*' three times '... Mayday *Lulubelle* in position [bearing and distance from a fixed mark or, simply, 'close to Nab Tower'] am sinking ... over.'

An urgent message calling for immediate aid should be prefixed 'Pan Pan Pan', then 'All stations [three times] ... this is *Lulubelle* in position ... medical assistance for crewman unconscious with multiple injuries ... over.'

Unless safety of life is involved the coastguard will prefer to work on Channel 67. In the vicinity of a local rescue involving several ships Channel 6 is recognized.

Urgent messages affecting all ships in a given area (e.g. a wreck, unlit buoy, suspected mine adrift) will be prefixed 'Securité' pronounced *say-cure-it-ay*. They are usually but not necessarily originated by shore stations.

(c) *Ship-shore personal messages*

To hook into the British Telecom network, contact any shore station and request a Link Call. You will be switched to a working channel, then say:

'Yankee Tango Delta' meaning it's a yacht telephone debit call which is to be charged to ... (telephone number). 'Link Call please to ... [area code and number being called] Over.'

It's convenient, and not all that expensive if you keep it short. Normally the shore station will tell you at the end what duration the call is being charged for.

It is also possible to have messages sent from a private telephone via any shore radio station. They will usually hold them until after the morning and evening weather messages on VHF when you hear 'Traffic for ... and ...', or it may be ten or more. The messages are dealt with in sequence.

Coastguard Rescue Centres

Stornoway 0851 2013 (01 10)
Oban 0631 63720 (02 40)
Clyde 0475 29988 (00 20)
Belfast 0247 883184 (03 05)
Ramsey 0624 813255 (03 50)
Liverpool 051-931 3343 (02 10)
Holyhead 0407 2051 (02 35)
Milford Haven 06465 218 (03 35)
Swansea 0792 66534 (00 05)
Hartland 02374 641 (01 20)
Falmouth 0326 317575 (01 40)
Brixham 08045 58292 (00 50)
Portland 0305 820441 (02 20)
Solent 0705 552100 (00 46)
Shetland 0595 2976 (01 05)
Pentland 0856 3268 (01 35)
Moray 0779 74278 (00 10)
Aberdeen 0224 592334 (03 20)
Forth 0333 50666 (02 05)
Tyne Tees 091 257 2691 (01 50)
Humber 0964 650351 (03 40)
Yarmouth 0493 851338 (00 40)
Thames 02556 5518 (02 50)
Dover 0304 210008 (01 05)

CG Stations' telephone numbers. Times in brackets are start of 4-hourly weather forecasts on Ch 67 – after calling on Ch 16

(d) *Keeping in touch*

When setting out to go farther afield than your local cruising ground, call up the nearest coastal radio station and make a 'Tango Romeo' message which says who you are, whereabouts, whither bound and what ETA. This will help the SAR organization in case you are overdue for any reason. Check in by R/T if you happen to pass any coastguard stations and sign off at the end of the voyage, when any messages awaiting you will be relayed.

Even yachts without R/T should take the precaution of calling their nearest Coastguard Rescue Centre by shore telephone. There are 25 of them all round the coasts of the British Isles as shown on the chart (p. 83) with their telephone numbers alongside each one.

There is a voluntary Coastguard Yacht and Boat Safety scheme which involves getting a form from any issuing authority, filling in all the data about yourself and your boat to help a search and rescue operation if and when it may be required. Coastguard stations, marinas, yacht clubs and Harbour Offices are mostly issuing authorities and have a red and blue circular sticker saying so.

In a cruising yacht there is much to be said for having an auto-pilot controlling the tiller or wheel to keep the boat on a steady pre-set course or at a given apparent wind angle. Under most conditions 'George' will do a better job than a helmsman, who can thus be freed to take shelter under the dodger, go below to put on a fix, make a hot drink or attend to an adjustment in the sail-plan without having to worry about an involuntary gybe or being taken aback.

In a well-balanced boat with a reasonably long keel it has always been possible to take a turn around the tiller with the bitter end of the jib-sheet and let the boat sail herself for long periods.

Running sufficiently far off the wind, which is to say when it is blowing from within 30° either side of dead astern, a very simple self-steering rig can be improvised as soon as you switch to a double headsail rig set wing-and-wing. Never mind if you don't have two headstays; the second jib can be set flying, then drop the main. Alternatively it might be possible to reef the main to approximately the same area as the winged-out headsail and regard the main boom as a second spinnaker pole, but it will need lazy guys to avoid coming up all-standing on a shroud. Thereafter follow the advice given in Colin Mudie and Patrick Ellam's hilarious book *Sopranino*, the account of how they showed the world that offshore distance races in boats under 20ft LOA were perfectly possible. That led to the Junior Offshore Group and such events as the Mini Transat, the race from UK to Antigua in boats under 6m LOA (21ft).

Here's how they rigged up their self-steering gear for sailing in the Trade Winds, once making a day's run of 134 miles in the process.

Instead of having foreguys led to the eyes of the boat and each separately secured, they had an endless foreguy from the outboard end of one boom through a swivel-block at the stem-head and back to the outboard end of the other boom. For adjusting this part of the rig, the guy was not secured there, but led back through a snatch-block to a cleat on or near the mast. The after guys from each boom were then led through blocks and secured to the tiller.

Thus when the wind exerted more pressure on the leeward headsail, causing the boat to luff up, the weather after guy would be hauling the tiller up to weather, thus pushing the ship's head offwind until the whole system was in equilibrium once more.

They had separate tiller lines rove off athwartships to limit the travel of the tiller and others incorporating heavy-duty shock cord to act as dampers.

On a reach they borrowed a variation of the Braine gear, which can be seen on most model yachts.

But for going to windward for long distances across the ocean something more sophisticated is required than tiller lines linked to the clews of headsails. Planning for the Single-Handed Transatlantic Race from Plymouth to New York in 1960 was just the impetus needed for the fertile minds of Francis Chichester and Colonel Blondie Hasler to lick the problem of keeping a small boat sailing efficiently to weather without having someone at the helm around the clock. Both came up with a vane on the transom which could be pre-set at a given apparent wind angle and directly linked to the rudder (or a trim tab). A quadrant at the base of the wind-vane had cross-over tiller lines so rigged that a tendency to bear away pulled the tiller to weather, and vice versa. There

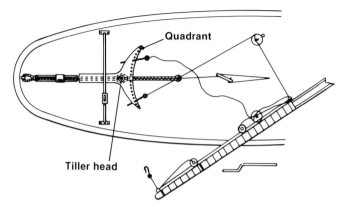

Braine's self-steering gear for model yachts

were many variations on the theme, but the most popular was marketed as the Hasler Self-Steering Gear.

When Blondie reached New York 48 days out in his 26ft junk-rigged Folkboat she had sailed herself for all but one hour of the voyage and set the fashion for all solo navigators or those sailing singlehanded.

While vane-steering has the supreme attribute of not calling for any source of power other than the wind, it has some drawbacks. It is vulnerable to damage either by the seas or while berthing. And it can hardly be said to enhance the appearance of a boat. There are more compact versions of his original idea still available today for the owner who does not want to depend on electrical power. They cost around £1,000, depending on the mounting brackets.

Modern Wind Vane steering attached to transom

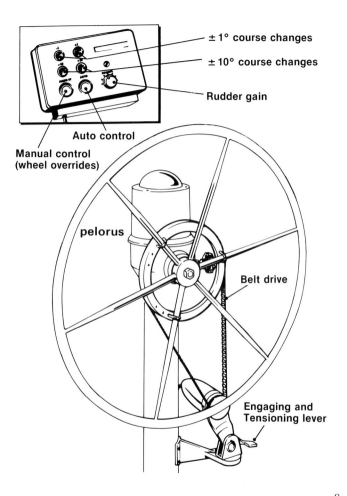

± 1° course changes

± 10° course changes

Rudder gain

Auto control

Manual control
(wheel overrides)

pelorus

Belt drive

Engaging and
Tensioning lever

Auto-pilots

Whereas power-assisted auto-pilots have been standard in most motorboats whose owners aim to do more than tow waterskiers behind them, they have only taken off for sailing yachts in the past decade. One UK firm has supplied 180,000 units in that time and is still selling 1,500 annually.

It started with a simple athwartships push-pull rod snapped on to a stud on the tiller arm, taking its command from an ordered course monitored by its own transmitting compass (see p. 88).

A simple variation for wheel steering involves a toothed rubber band-drive engaged to an inner sprocket secured to the ship's steering wheel, driven by its own control unit, usually mounted low down on the pedestal of the pelorus (see left), or on the side of the cockpit. There is a simple tensioning lever for engaging the band-drive effectively.

Many feel that the need for an ordered course to steer in degrees throws up discrepancies with the steering compass. It is simple to put the boat on the desired course and then hit the 'auto' button on the control unit. Adjustments can be made in 1° or 10° steps by pressing other buttons. Even the rudder action can be damped to suit your own boat's steering behaviour. To disengage, there is a 'stand-by' button; or you simply lift the piston unit off its locking stud on the tiller.

If you want, the control panel can be duplicated by another on a remote lead. Also there is the option of a small wind vane to sail by apparent wind angle. Finally, there is a black box which will link the controls to any radio navigation system (Decca or Loran-C) and take you to the next way-point.

In case the auto-pilot forgets itself, there is an off-course alarm system and overload protection. In all systems there is an upper limit to the weight of impact on the rudder the auto-pilot can handle. This is known as the 'stall thrust'. Each model has its designed limits, coupled with the maximum size

Control buttons

Piston drive

Spigot on tiller

Modern autohelm with fluxgate compass built into control arm

Piston arm snapped onto tiller

Fluxgarte compass – knob on top for setting desired course

Earlier autosteering model

of boat it can handle. Makers vary in their claims for these limits. One has at the bottom end of its range a stall thrust of 160lb (73kg), suitable for boats up to 33ft (10m). Recently I have sailed a Nicholson 36 with this same auto-pilot and found it did a fine job, although possibly the onset of limiting sea states and awkward wind angles came rather sooner than would the next model up the line: 300lb (136kg) stall thrust, suitable for boats up to 43ft (13m).

Another manufacturer offers to drive a 33ft boat with $12\frac{1}{2}\%$ less thrust for a 42ft boat. Here is another case for talking to an independent dealer or consultant.

Like most of today's advanced technology for boats, prices have come down with competition. The simplest push-pull system for a tiller costs a little over £200, while the wheel steering auto-pilot is under £400, surprisingly less than for a typical wind-operated vane steering.

The heart of these auto-pilots is a small gimballed fluxgate compass, no bigger than a golf ball. It is not a north-seeking magnetic compass in the conventional sense but keeps pointing to whatever relative heading is pre-set by the operator. The guts of it looks like an armature winding.

Power requirements

Whichever way you slice it, auto-pilots need electrical power behind them. It is safe to say that their average consumption is equivalent to having your navigation lights switched on. Nevertheless, if you don't keep a second battery isolated for starting your engine, you can flatten a battery overnight by running under auto-pilot with navigation lights switched on and no restrictions below. That is why a Beneteau 32 in which I was a guest last year had to sail into the lock at Ouistreham after an easy passage from Beaulieu, then hump the battery ashore for recharging and a long expensive lunch before going on to Caen. I recommend two 60 amp-hr batteries with a

**Wind generator,
taffrail mounted**

simple selector switch enabling either or both to be put on load.

As any submariner will tell you, the signs of a DC battery at the top of its charge are that it should be gassing freely and show maximum voltage and electrolyte specific density readings (using a hygrometer). In a yacht there is generally only a voltmeter to indicate your battery's health. Once below 12V (or 24V, as the case may be) smack it on charge right away. A safe rule is to run the engine for an hour twice a day, even if your hotel load (fridge, lighting and navigation aids) is not restricted by the skipper's edict, which sometimes stretches to crossing the Channel with navigation lights switched off.

Other sources of power independent of fossil fuels are the sun and wind. A typical single solar energy plate in direct sunlight will give you about a 3amp charge, but it costs nearly £700 and does not offer to perform often in British waters during months such as August 1985, 1986 or 1987.

A wind generator, which is a mini-windmill stuck on its own mast at the taffrail, will deliver 2amps or 12V in a steady 12kt breeze rising to 6amps in 30kt winds at an installation cost of around £400. But it depends on relative wind strength, so may not be too effective in that dream cruise to Antigua along the edge of the Doldrums. One model can double as a towed water turbine, especially suitable for fast downwind sailing in low relative wind speeds.

Most occasional yacht navigators are put off enlisting the aid of the sun or the stars, let alone the moon or the planets, to fix their position by the very thought of trying to understand the theory behind the practice. Words like Sidereal Hour Angle, the ephemerides or the First Point of Aries and the rest of the jargon are daunting hurdles to be faced in a class-room, let alone in the wet cockpit of a yacht.

But you don't have to understand the theory of internal combustion engines to drive a car, or how a microprocessor works to check your bank balance at an external cash-point. All you need to know are their modes of operation, their snags and practical limitations – and learn Osram's Law ('switch it on', first propounded by the Pakistani physicist, Professor O.S. Ram).

So, before you turn your back on a sextant and those over-crowded tables in a nautical almanac, which are about as confusing to read as a Southern Region commuter time-table, join me in putting celestial navigation to work without relying on too much of the theory.

Which Sextant?

This instrument, so-called because they used always to have a 60° graduated arc for reading off the altitude, will measure the observed angle above the horizon of the sun, moon or any other heavenly body and give the answer in degrees, minutes and seconds of arc (in practice, minutes and decimals: thus 33° 47.7′ is 33 degrees 47 minutes and 42 seconds).

Don't rush in and blow up to £350 on the sort of alloy-framed sextant a U-boat commander used. Pause to determine what you really need from it. That in turn depends on the confidence you place in any altitude you measure under the

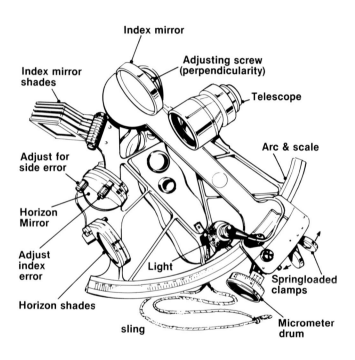

Professional sextant

Index mirror

Index mirror shades

Adjusting screw (perpendicularity)

Telescope

Adjust for side error

Arc & scale

Horizon Mirror

Adjust index error

Light

Springloaded clamps

Horizon shades

sling

Micrometer drum

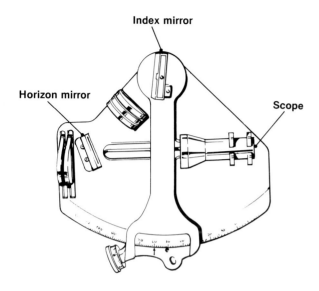

Index mirror

Horizon mirror

Scope

Beginner's sextant (solid plastic)

You pay for what you get and, in some cases, what you do not need. The simplest and by far the cheapest is a sextant constructed around a flat heavy-duty plastic plate cut as the segment of a circle with 120° on its graduated lower arc. The index arm and its associated mirror rotate about the 'centre' of the imaginary circle, with a micrometer for fine reading of minutes of arc after having spring-locked the index arm on to the nearest degree. It costs less than £30 and is quite adequate for all the purposes listed above within the following limitations:

(a) Its claimed accuracy is one minute, probably within the operating error of most beginners.

(b) Its telescope has only 1.5 magnification and a limited field of view, so locking on to and bringing stars down to the horizon will be that much more difficult.

(c) It is susceptible to considerable errors of alignment and must be checked on each occasion of use. (See below for sextant errors.) One I picked up the other day had so much side error that the direct and reflected images of the sun never met.

(d) It has no built-in lighting for reading off observed altitudes at dusk. But since you won't be relying on star sights, this inconvenience is acceptable.

(e) It has a limited set of shades (hinged filters which can be swung into your field of vision through either mirror to reduce glare).

Otherwise it serves its purpose and comes securely stowed within its own plastic box about 8in square and 3in deep. The sextant itself weights a little over a pound (0.75kg).

Second-hand sextants
These are surprisingly hard to come by, considering the decline in the Merchant Navy. Occasionally the classified

conditions prevailing at sea in a yacht. Start with the firm intention that you will never waste your time taking sights when conditions are such that their results are of dubious value right from the first step; that is in measuring the observed altitude. Master the sun shot in good conditions first before you even think about trying out a set of stars. Know what degree of confidence to invest in your efforts, always erring on the sceptical side.

columns of a local newspaper in one of our seaports will have one, but the yachting press rarely advertise them. When they do, the more sophisticated professional models fetch between £75–£150 if bought direct, probably more from a chandler.

What to look for:

(a)   Check both mirrors and the telescope for signs of damp. The mirrors can always be resilvered at little cost. If you leave blotchy patches on them the efficiency of the sextant falls off quickly.

(b)   There should be a test certificate inside the lid of the box with the date and maximum error obtaining – usually negligible.

(c)   Check for the errors listed below and be sure that the adjusting screws for eradicating them are operable.

(d)   See that the lighting circuit is functioning.

(e)   The sextant should be clamped in its stowage inside its box so that it does not rattle around when it is picked up.

(f)   Make sure that the spring lock holds the index arm firmly on to the graduated arc.

(g)   Go for a telescope with 3 × or 5 × magnification but don't bother with 8 × 30 monocular star scopes which cannot cope with the amount of movement usually prevailing.

Correcting errors

Its accuracy depends on:

(a)   Certain errors being allowed for or mechanically adjusted out of the way.

(b)   Various corrections to allow for the observer's height of eye (above sea level) tabulated in your almanac.

(c)   Special corrections for moon, planet or star shots, also from the tables.

(d)   Having a reliable distant horizon from which to measure the altitude. Since an error of one minute of arc can

work its way on to your plotted position as one nautical mile, it is important to take all these into account, but especially the quality of the horizon. On a calm clear day with a sharp horizon easily showing where the sea ends and the sky begins and little or no movement on the boat there is no problem. But a hazy horizon and a watery sun observed from a bucking platform is where you must trust your own judgement on the attainable accuracy. Not only must you find the true horizon, if necessary waiting for the boat to lift on top of the swell, but the angle measured must be in the vertical plane. Your eye looks at the horizon through the lower glass, which has a mirror to one side picking up the body to be observed through the index mirror, so called because it is attached to the index arm on which the altitude measured is read in degrees and minutes.

In practice with the sun it is easy to swing the index arm in the direction of the reflected path of the sun on the surface until you have the lower limb (bottom edge) of the sun roughly on the horizon. Waggle the sextant from side to side until your observed lower limb just kisses the horizon (see p. 93) with an unchanged altitude setting.

If you are timing the sight, as you must for all but meridian passage shots (the moment when the observed body hangs stationary in the sky, generally nearing due south neither climbing nor falling), call 'cut' or 'mark' or whatever you have as agreed drill with your assistant or, if you are using a stopwatch, press it for subsequent correlating with GMT (in our sailing season and UK waters this will be British Summer Time minus 1 hour).

In the days before inertial navigation and hyperbolic aids, aircraft navigators used 'bubble' sextants with their own artificial horizon, but they are not stable enough for our purposes and are no longer available. On the eve of a Bermuda Race in pre-Loran-C days a hot ocean racing navigator showed me

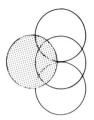

Checking side error by taking the reflected sun through the observed one

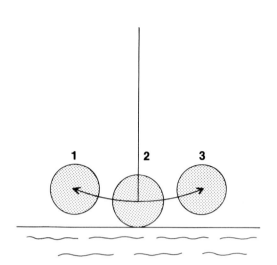

Slewing the sextant to get maximum altitude with the sextant vertical.

his special sextant with a pre-spun gyro inside its handle that forcibly restrained him if he tried measuring altitudes off the plumb vertical. When next seen after the usual broad reach down to Bermuda, he was making his landfall under spinnaker from the sou'west, having missed the island on his first pass.

The other errors must all be allowed for or corrected in this order:

Perpendicularity is a check to confirm that the index mirror is lying in the same plane as the sextant. Set the index arm around 60° against the scale on its arc and then look obliquely into the index mirror at the index arc and its reflected image. If they don't form an uninterrupted line there is perpendicularity error which must be taken out by adjusting a set-screw on the back of the index mirror.

Side error occurs when the reflected and direct image of the sun are not in the same plane, due to the horizon glass being slightly out of plane. To check it, use as much colour filter as you need to look straight at the sun, set the index arm on zero and turn the micrometer first one way and then the other. In the process the sun's reflected image will pass from above to below. If the reflective image does not coincide precisely with the direct sun (see above) the side error can be taken out by turning a screw in the centre of the frame of the horizon glass.

Index error is present if the horizon glass is not parallel to the index glass when the sextant is set to read 0°00′. The simplest way of checking this is to look at any distant horizontal datum, such as the horizon, when it will be seen to have a step in, as in focusing with a modern camera. Turn the micrometer until the horizon forms a clean unbroken line.

Horizon broken with sextant reading zero.

Then it will be seen that the index arm is reading a small amount either side of zero.

If it is to the *left* of the zero point, the error is said to be 'on the arc' and the correction to be applied when reading off any observed altitude is *minus*.

If the index arm is to the *right* of zero, it is 'off the arc' and the amount has to be *added* to the observed altitude.

If the amount is small (under 3 minutes) let it stand and just remember to apply it on all occasions. If it is a relatively large figure it should be eliminated by an adjusting screw at the base of the horizon glass frame. An index error of

Horizon straight. Index error 2° off the arc (+)

1.5 minutes can be lived with, just so long as you remember that it represents $1\frac{1}{2}$ nautical miles' error on your position line.

The above method is best checked by taking several observations breaking and then re-aligning the horizon.

In theory the most accurate method of finding index error is to eliminate side error as described above and then measure the sun's observed diameter as follows:

Reflected image above and under observed sun.

1 Get the reflected image sitting tangentally on top of the observed sun and read off the number of minutes on the arc.

2 Swing the reflected image down until it is now tangentally *under* the observed sun and read off the minutes off the arc.

What you have done is measured twice the diameter of the sun. The sun's monthly pages in the almanac give a lot of data: *inter alia*, its meridian passage, times of rising and setting and twilight and the measurement of the sun's *semi-diameter* for each day, which varies between 15.8 and 16.3 minutes. (The reason it is listed is that the tables are computed on the assumption that you should be observing the *centre* of the sun and not its upper or lower limb).

So your reading for index error should add up to 4 times the semi-diameter, e.g.:

If the sun's semi-diameter is listed as 15.8, its full diameter is 31.6 minutes and the sum total of your reading on and off the arc should amount to 63.2. The amount by which the two readings are biased either side of zero on the scale is your index error. Suppose you read 30.0 on the arc and 33.5 off it (totalling 63.5, which is near enough). Divide the total measured by two ($=31.8$) and you will see that the real zero point is $33.5 - 31.8$ *off the arc* $= 1.7$ minutes, and your index error is $+1.7$.

Looking after the sextant

Whether it cost you £40 or £400, a sextant which is not cared for will soon reduce your self-confidence in the observations you take with it. Here are the do's and don'ts:

1　Have a permanent purpose-built stowage for your sextant case, preferably so that the lid can be opened and the instrument taken out or replaced *in situ*. It should be located in the driest part of the boat consistent with accessibility.

2　Never grab the sextant or use it except by its handle.

3　Keep it secured to your person by a lanyard round your neck to the handle.

4　Have a loose fitting plastic or other waterproof hood which you can slip over the sextant while exposed on deck and not actually shooting sights.

5　Dry it off immediately after use, as gently as you can. Use lens paper to clean the mirrors and telescope; soft tissue for the frame of the instrument.

6　Keep the graduated arc lightly oiled.

7　Check the various errors on each occasion before use.

8　Have your telescope eyepiece focus point marked in some way so that no time is wasted looking through a blurred scope.

Times

At this point you need a broad understanding of the significance of the various kinds of time used in celestial navigation.

GMT remains the datum time from which all celestial navigation calculations are derived.

Zone Time is an arbitrary adjustment of clock time to spread the hours of darkness more or less evenly either side of midnight. With a few exceptions (Iran $3\frac{1}{2}$ hours ahead of GMT, Newfoundland $3\frac{1}{2}$ hours behind) these adjustments are made in units of one hour, representing $15°$ of longitude spread $7\frac{1}{2}°$ either side of the meridian in the centre of each Time Zone. So GMT extends from longitude $7°30'W$. Bermuda in the vicinity of $65°W$ lies in the zone either side of $60°W$ ($52°30W$ to $67°30W$) which is 4 hours behind GMT.

Local Time is Zone Time corrected to take account of any local variations such as Summer Time, usually one hour added to give longer evenings. For cruising around the UK with the continental NW European countries all basically on Zone (-1) (i.e. keeping 1 hour ahead of GMT) this is usually simple to keep straight in one's mind. All of them keep Summer Time, but there is the maddening complication that not all countries move on to Summer Time or off it on the same date, although the EEC has promised to iron out this anomaly. It is more a source of getting local tidal predictions wrong than any threat to working out celestial navigation problems.

Ship's Time is simply the time kept on the ship's clock which governs the change of watches and meal times. On a long W–E passage there is always some competition among the watchkeepers for when the crossing of each Time Zone should be put into effect (the equitable solution is to shave $\frac{1}{2}$ hour off each of two night watches). Most airline passengers adjust their wristwatches on take-off to the local time of the next stopover, but round-trip commuters to New York by Concorde resolutely keep London time in the eternal battle to stave off 'jet-lag'.

Greenwich Hour Angle (GHA) is an east-to-west measurement of the sun's position relative to the Greenwich meridian as seen from the earth's centre at any given moment. It is tabulated from 0°–360° for every 1 or 2 hours on the monthly sun pages in any almanac, with corrections for intervening times.

At 1400 GMT the GHA of the sun on 14 January 1987 was 31°08.3. If the time of observation had been 15.11.42 the sun's GHA correction table for 1hr 11mins 42 is 17°55.5, making the GHA at that time 31°08.3 + 17°55.0 = 49°03.3.

Local Hour Angle (LHA) is the Hour Angle measured from the longitude on which the observer happens to be, also measured in degrees to the westward (or clockwise around the globe). LHA is found by:

If your longitude is West, *adding* it to the GHA. If your longitude is East, *subtracting* it from the GHA.

Hereabouts use a little ploy with 360° (or multiples) being a wild card to be added or subtracted as necessary to make the sum fit the tables.

In an E longitude 360° can be deducted if the LHA comes to over 360°.

In a W longitude 360° may be added to the GHA if needed to give a high enough figure for subtraction.

Other definitions
Geographical Position (GP) is the spot on the earth's surface directly under any heavenly body, assuming a line drawn from it to the earth's centre.

The GP at any given moment can be measured EW by its LHA and NS by its Declination:

Declination (Dec) is the latitude of the GP N or S of the equator. In the case of the sun, when it is furthest away from those of us who sail in northern waters, it will reach latitude 23°S in mid-winter and about six months later reach latitude 23°N. As the sun crosses the equator with declination zero we have the spring and autumn equinoxes (equal period of daylight and night) usually associated with equinoctial gales, although it seems to me there is little more truth in that assertion than saying it is always rough in the Bay of Biscay. In nautical almanacs the declination is said to have the *same name* as the latitude when both are N or S; but a *contrary name* when they are not (e.g. Lat 40°N dec 12°S is a *contrary name*).

Zenith Distance (ZD) When you measure the altitude of the sun it is the angle observed between the horizon and the sun after making various corrections already noted. For the purpose of calculating one's latitude from a noon sight, it is necessary to work from the complement of your observed altitude: 90° minus altitude, since we have to deal with a latitude scale running from 0° at the equator to 90° at the pole, and not the other way round.

Azimuth is the true bearing of any heavenly body. It can most accurately be determined by special alt-azimuth tables, but may also be obtained by visual observation if the altitude is not too high.

Taking a sight and working it out
Books, tables and methods
To work out a celestial sight (or 'reduce it', as they say), there are certain publications which you must have, unless you have a programmed computer to do the job for you. Those most commonly found on the navigator's shelf are:

NP 314   The *Nautical Almanac* for the current year. Same title in USA.
AP 3270   *Sight Reduction Tables for Air Navigation*
NP 401   *Sight Reduction Tables for Marine Navigation*
         (3) covers latitudes 30°–45° N and S. Jacksonville to Halifax.
         (4) covers latitudes 45°–60° N and S. The British Isles. Bordeaux to Bergen.
HO 249 US equivalent sight reduction tables (Now known as Pub 249).
Reed's Nautical Almanac for the current year.
Macmillan & Silk Cut Nautical Almanac for the current year.
Macmillan & Silk Cut Yachtsman's Handbook.

Depending on which tables you use there are various pads of Sight Reduction forms which keep your calculations moving step-by-step in an orderly manner. The Admiralty's NP 400(a) is suitable for use with any of them. *Reed's* and *Macmillan* both have sharply different methods of presenting their tables which may seem unfamiliar at first, but are explained in the text.

Use of Calculators
There are many different methods of reducing sights by using hand-held scientific calculators to produce all the answers without the chore of having to enter too many tables, add up or subtract.

The simplest is the Simanda Astro-Navigation Kit* which gives you a sextant of sorts, a scientific calculator, *Reed's Almanac* and a readily comprehensible step-by-step guide on how to do it – all for less than £50. If you already have a sextant and *Reed's*, the calculator and the methodology cost just £15.

Nursery slopes – two sights to master
(1) *Meridian Altitude – the noon sight* The first and easiest sight is to measure the sun's altitude at the moment of its meridian passage: that is when it crosses your meridian of longitude either due north or due south of you. You can work out when this will happen by reference to the monthly Sun tables in the Nautical Astronomy section of *Reed's Almanac* or other almanacs and in Admiralty or US equivalents. It is listed as either 'Transit' or 'Mer-Pass'. Since Greenwich Mean Time is an average based on 24 hours for each 365 days of the year, meridian passage seldom occurs precisely at noon GMT even on the meridian of Greenwich, which lies N-S roughly between Newhaven and the fairway into Le Havre. The tables show the sun's meridian passage can be a few minutes (up to 14) early or late on 1200 GMT.

Having obtained the time of Mer-Pass, say, 1208, then you must correct it for whatever distance you happen to be located yourself off the prime meridian. To do this, convert arc of longitude into time by the simple formula that each degree is equivalent to 4 minutes of time. If you are to the east of Greenwich you will get Mer-Pass early, as indeed you get sunrise earlier as you fly towards Hong Kong from Heathrow. If, for example, you are off Falmouth in longitude 5°W your correction will be 5 × 4 = 20 minutes later and your time of meridian passage will be 1208 + 20 = 1228 GMT (or

* Obtainable from Simanda Yachting Services, 8 Grovelands, Lower Bourne, Farnham, Surrey GU10 3RQ.

1328 BST). There are converting tables in the almanacs for arc into time, in case the above is beyond the scope of your mental abacus or pocket calculator.

A Mer-Alt shot as it is called is easier to hit off if you have the time of its happening worked out beforehand, but it is not necessary. Nor need you worry if your estimated position is doubtful, since you need to be over 15 minutes of longitude out before you affect the issue by a minute of time. In the case quoted above you'd have to be west of the Lizard to be a minute late on your prediction. Often it is necessary to get the helmsman to come off course, (either to get the spinnaker or jib out of the sextant's field of view or, simply, to allow the navigator to take his sight without being doused by heavy spray). So an accurate prediction of the time of meridian passage is helpful.

Sextant altitude at meridian passage.
1 Sun's image before meridian passage
2 At meridian passage
3 Shortly after meridian passage with altitude decreasing

It is not strictly necessary, because you can get your sight by watching the sun's altitude climb and slow down briefly to hang stationary in the sky before the altitude starts to drop again (see above). You just read the altitudes until you have passed their peak, then take the time and log reading.

Bringing it back alive Since you'll need both hands to use the sextant, first brace yourself securely standing up so that you can bring the sun down clear of the rig. Leaning back against the main boom is one option, but *always* clip on with a safety harness, even in calm weather. It is surprising how much uneven movement a boat has in calm seas. A friend of mine lost his life taking a noon shot on a westward trade wind crossing to the Caribbean. An unseen, lazy swell caught the boat and her navigator off-balance. The motor did not start first touch, and there was so little wind that the watch on deck could not lower the drooping spinnaker and get back to him soon enough.

Sometimes it pays to have another member of the crew hold on to you as you take the sight.

Before taking the sight, determine your height of eye at the moment of shooting (usually 10–12 feet in a typical yacht). This will be used to enter the Total Altitude Correction Table to cover all sextant corrections except index error.

At 12ft and an observed altitude of 35° the correction for a lower limb (LL) shot will be + 11.4 (interpolated between 30° and 40°). If it was taken in June, July or August there is a further minuscule correction of − 0.2, making your final figure + 11.2.

Now the working is easy. For a sight taken in N latitudes:

Sextant altitude	36°07.8
Index error (say)	− 2.8
	36°05.0
LL alt correction	+ 11.2
Corrected altitude	36°16.2
ZD (90° − alt)	53°43.8
Dec N (same)	8°38.6
Latitude	62°22.4N

Note the final addition of 43.8 and 38.6 minutes ends up as 82.4, which is 1° carried forward and 22.4 minutes, there being 60 minutes to a degree. If the Dec had been S (contrary) it would have been subtracted from ZD making the latitude 45°05.2N.

That's all there is to it. The end result is that you have your latitude fixed beyond doubt within your personal error of sight-taking and any errors you have not properly taken out of the sextant itself (see p. 92). Even amongst skilled navigators in perfect conditions individual errors can amount to 0.75 minutes, which is $\frac{3}{4}$ mile.

(2) *Sun Sight – the Single Position line* This will put you on a line at right angles to the bearing (azimuth) of the sun, somewhere on which your position lies. On its own it's no better than a single compass bearing of a known feature on the coastline.

The data required before reducing the sight are:

(a) Your DR position at the time of taking the sight. This need not be very accurate.
(b) The True Altitude (H_o) of your sextant shot after applying all the necessary corrections, as in taking the Mer-Alt sight.
(c) The time (GMT) at which the sight was taken accurate to ±2secs, well within the scope of any quartz crystal watch with a recent time-check behind it.
(d) For future reference, but not needed for the working, note the log reading and the bearing of the sun.
(e) The assumed latitude, rounded off to the degree nearest to your DR latitude.
(f) The assumed longitude needed to round off the computation of LHA so as to get rid of its minutes of arc. This may be some distance from your DR longitude but don't worry, it'll all come out in the wash.

(g) The Declination appropriate for the GMT of the sight.

The sextant altitude used must be precisely on the GMT at which it was taken. The best way is to take several shots, each carefully timed, and end up with an ironed-out average. This introduces an area of potential error which does not apply to Mer Alt sights, in which the altitude is read off when the sun has stopped ascending, and no time is needed.

If possible, always use the same crew member to note the times of your shots. It sounds simple enough, but it is surprising how many people get flustered and make silly mistakes. It is better not to let your timekeeper use his own watch, but either give him one with a known error from a recent time-signal or, better still, a stopwatch.

All he has to do is wait for you to say 'Stand by . . . cut!' (or 'mark!' in an American boat), then write down the time in minutes and seconds, followed by the sextant angle in degrees and minutes of arc to a single place of decimals as called by you. Always make him repeat the sextant altitude back to you before going on to take the next altitude, which again is noted against the time. How many observations you take for a single sight is dependent on the quality of the horizon and your own confidence. Unless the cloud cover or sea conditions make me accept less, I never take fewer than three shots.

The most popular way of averaging out altitudes and times is by adding them both up and dividing by the number of observations, probably using a calculator. But the best way is to plot all of them against their times on squared paper, as in the diagram on page 100. To do this the timekeeper starts his stopwatch at the first 'cut!', which is later plotted as an x against zero time, with the others then plotted out against stopwatch time in the same manner. Then draw a straight line which most closely caters for all the x-marks on the graph paper. From it you can choose any convenient altitude and time as inputs for working out the sight.

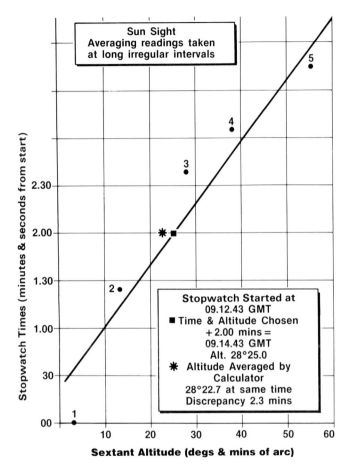

Sun Sight
Averaging readings taken at long irregular intervals

Stopwatch Times (minutes & seconds from start)

Sextant Altitude (degs & mins of arc)

Stopwatch Started at
09.12.43 GMT
■ **Time & Altitude Chosen**
+ 2.00 mins =
09.14.43 GMT
Alt. 28°25.0
✳ **Altitude Averaged by**
Calculator
28°22.7 at same time
Discrepancy 2.3 mins

First you have to check the GMT of your stopwatch zero by stopping it against a time signal or clock of known accuracy.

The example in the diagram shows that the altitude chosen to work from is 2.3 minutes of arc at variance with the one which a calculator would have arrived at by averaging out the 'cuts'. The reason is that the calculator took each altitude at face value and included one wild one which was obviously inaccurate, whereas the line drawn across the graph paper ignored that one. In some cases that could mean a discrepancy of over 2 miles in the position line and, therefore, the fix ultimately obtained with a second sight later.

Working it out
Using modern tables it is no more difficult than reconciling your chequebook stubs against your bank balance. If you use a sight reduction form, it is even easier. The following is an abridged form, since the corrections to time and sextant altitude are assumed to have been done in your head or on a scratch-pad.

Date	15 July 19—	
DR position	49°48 N	05°42 W
GMT	08h. 46m 01s	The time has been averaged out and any corrections applied.
GHA sun	298° 32.1′	Taken from *Nautical Almanac* for exact hour = 0800.
Increment	11° 30.0′	From Sun GHA Correction tables for 46mins 01secs.
GHA	310° 02.1′	
Assumed longitude (W)	6° 02.1′	Long. W is subtracted; E is added. The assumed longitude
LHA sun ·	304° 00.0′	arbitrarily chosen near the DR

		so as to end up with LHA reading in degrees only, no minutes of arc.
Assumed latitude 50° N		Nearest exact latitude to the DR.
Declination	N 21° 35.2′	From *Nautical Almanac*, interpolating d between Decs for successive days.
Tab alt(H_c)	38° 01.7′	See note on increments below.
True alt(H_o)	37° 54.9′	All corrections applied, inc height of eye for tables.
Intercept	6.8′ Away	In this case H_c is the greater, otherwise it would be Towards.
Azimuth (bearing) 102°		
Log reading, say 62.8		Co:125° Sp:7kts (Var)

Increments The small 'd' which crops up in the tables is for the difference between successive entries. In some cases the figure is so small that you can allow for it by eye. In this case the Dec for 0800 is N21°35.6; for 1000 it is N21°34.9, a difference of only 0.7′. But 'd' is a significant factor in arriving at the Tab Alt(H_c). You first take out the altitude for the degrees of declination (N 21°) and must then adjust to take account of the 35.2′. The Alt-Az Tables as they are sometimes known are entered for the assumed latitude (50°N) in the same 'name' as the Declination (i.e. N), LHA of 304° against Dec of 21°. The information supplied is H_c37°35.8′ with d as +44.2 and the azimuth as 102°.

The d figure is simply the difference between Dec 21° and Dec 22°. There are interpolation tables with instructions which are comprehensible. Or use a calculator to work out how much of d+44.2 you have to apply for the 35.2′ of declination:

$$\frac{35.2}{60} \times 44.2 = 25.9$$

On obtaining the intercept, if the corrected observed altitude (H_o) is greater than the tabulated altitude (H_c), the intercept is *towards* the sun's azimuth shown above. If H_c is the greater the intercept is *away* from the sun's bearing. Just remember: 'True Greater Towards'.

Plotting the sight
(1) Plot the *assumed* latitude and longitude used in the working above.
(2) Draw the azimuth (bearing) from that lat-long position and mark off the intercept as miles using the latitude scale on the plot.
(3) A line drawn at right angles through the intercept point is your position line.

When you get your next sight, you can run it on, exactly as in a running fix using single compass bearings at intervals so spaced as to give you a cut of 30° or more. This will give you a sun-run-sun observed position or, more simply, a fix. The following example uses a meridan altitude sight as the second position line (see p. 102). The plot next to it is one taken on the 1984 Bermuda Race.

The Moon: a little more difficult
Because it is the fastest celestial body in the sky (at 2,400 mph), and its high rate of change of bearing and altitude call for fiddling corrections to the sextant readings, the moon is not everybody's favourite. But it's there, and on about 15 days each month available for a simultaneous shot with the sun. In fact, it is only when it is full that is never seen by day, since it rises around sunset and sets at dawn. During half the rest of the month it will appear as a waxing segment, getting steadily bigger from its first appearance as a sliver of a new moon, until it goes out as an old moon on the wane.

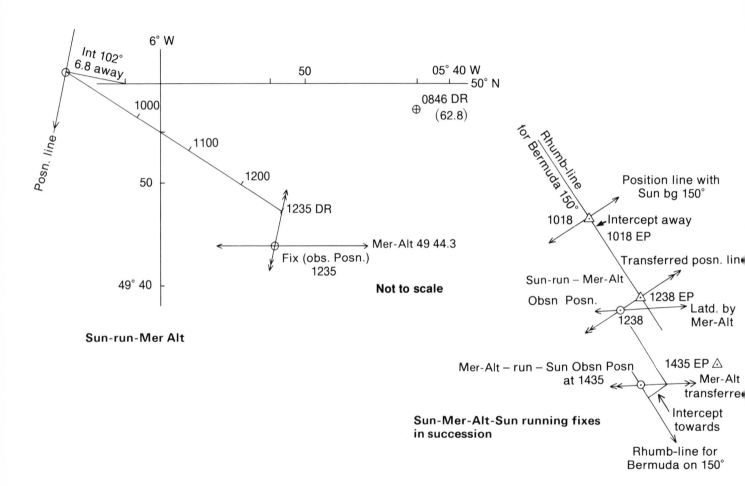

6° W

Int 102°
6.8 away

Posn. line

50

05° 40 W
50° N

0846 DR
(62.8)

1000

1100

1200

50

1235 DR

Mer-Alt 49 44.3

Fix (obs. Posn.)
1235

49° 40

Not to scale

Sun-run-Mer Alt

Rhumb-line
for Bermuda 150°

Position line with
Sun bg 150°

1018

Intercept away
1018 EP

Transferred posn. line

Sun-run – Mer-Alt

Obsn Posn.

1238 EP

Latd. by
Mer-Alt

1238

Mer-Alt – run – Sun Obsn Posn
at 1435

1435 EP

Mer-Alt
transferred

Intercept
towards

**Sun-Mer-Alt-Sun running fixes
in succession**

Rhumb-line for
Bermuda on 150°

102

To distinguish between the two, remember the italic letter *x*. The waxing moon comes first and has its clearly-defined visible edge to the right as you look at it. Once on the wane, its hard perimeter is on the left. The waxing half-moon rises around mid-day and has its meridian passage near sunset, so it is an ideal afternoon sight, when the sun is in the western part of the sky. The waning half-moon will be in its meridian about sunrise and set at noon, so is suitable for a simultaneous sun-moon shot in the forenoons.

The tables allow you to take an observation either when its Upper Limb is tangential to the horizon (and the rest of it below) or with the Lower Limb on the horizon, as in a normal sun sight. Near its various quarters the moon appears to be canted, so that it is necessary to take an Upper Limb sometimes to be sure of not getting a false altitude by measuring the partly hidden lower sector of the moon.

Because it is so much nearer to the earth, its relative movement is quicker than any other heavenly body, so accurate timekeeping and recording are essential. But you seldom have glare on the horizon from which you are measuring its altitude, so can usually shoot without shades over either mirror or the sextant telescope.

Given modern tables in the nautical almanacs, and special care in taking the sight, there is no reason why the Moon has traditionally been regarded as a fickle friend of yacht navigators.

All nautical almanacs have separate correction tables for Apparent Sextant Angle, GHA Moon and the Moon's Declination.

The GHA may be tabulated hourly, four times a day (*Reed's*) or three times a day (*Macmillan*). Suppose the moon was taken at nearly the same time as the sun shot in the example above, say, 08h.52m.23s on 15 July. Then

GHA for 0600 is	28°58.8′	with variation listed as 14° 30.3
add for 2 hours	+ 14°29.0′	(Moon GHA Corrn table for 1–6hrs)
for 52 mins	+ 12°34.0	(Moon GHA Corrn table for up to 1hr)
for 23 secs	+ 5.6′	
GHA for 08.52.23 is	56°07.4′	

When it comes to taking out the Declination, see by inspection of the tables whether the corrections should be added or subtracted, depending on whether the next figure is greater or lesser.

Declination for 0600	S 5°24.8′	16.6 variation per hour noted
Subtract for 2 hours 2 × 16.6	− 33.2′	
For 52m 23s	− 15.5′	(From Moon Dec Corrn tables)
Declination at 08h.52m23s is	S 4°36.1′	

Sextant Altitude Each almanac has its own system for applying Moon altitude total corrections to Apparent Altitude. They all have explanatory notes. First you must enter the monthly page for the Moon's times of rising and setting. There you will find the horizontal parallax figure for the day, probably between 54.1 and 61.0.

Then enter the Moon altitude table with the Observed Altitude (sextant altitude corrected for index error) and horizontal parallax figure, taking care to use the correct half of the page of Upper or Lower Limb. From that you get a correction + or − to Observed Altitude; then you must make a further correction to height of eye, since the tables have been computed for 100 feet above sea level and have a special correction table to bring the observation down to the height at which you took it. Thus:

The Moon's Upper Limb was taken at 08.52 on 15 July with 12ft height of eye (HE) as 24°50.0′. The horizontal parallax (HP) was 59.3.

Moon's UL	24°50.0′
Correction	+ 25.3′
HE	+ 6.4′
True alt	25°21.7′

From this point on, the working and plotting is the same as for a single position line from a sun sight.

Star Sights: counter-productive?

I rate simultaneous star shots at morning or evening twilight as not worth the bother. In ideal conditions – so rarely found in a yacht – a set of stars with Polaris (the feeble but easily-found North Star) and 3 other correctly identified stars will give you an instant fix of potentially high reliability; but typically you find yourself cold and wet on deck at night with five-eighths cloud and only fleeting glimpses of your pre-selected stars between douches of cold seawater.

Naturally the quality of the horizon degenerates quickly at dusk, while the stars themselves melt away at dawn. The whole business of sitting around waiting to fire from the hip is tedious not only for the navigator but also for his chosen timekeeper. Then there follows the chore of working it all out. Robin Knox-Johnston sailed 27,000 miles around the world in 313 days without taking a star sight except on rare occasions for fun or to pass the time.

If you are determined, or curious, to find out for yourself, there is no better book on the subject than Mary Blewitt's *Celestial Navigation for Yachtsmen*, first published in the reign of George VI but constantly updated, excepting only that the target reader implied by the title has not been changed to Yachtspersons. Her examples are all worked using the *Nautical Almanac* and AP 3270 – *Sight Reduction Tables for Air Navigation*, Vol I.

The Sextant as a Rangefinder

The sextant can also be brought on deck for other uses than hacking down celestial bodies. It is by far the most accurate rangefinder available on board. Given the height of a lighthouse or daymark you can read off the vertical sextant angle and refer to any almanac for a conversion table giving range. A simultaneous bearing of the object yields an accurate and instantaneous fix. The tables are intended for use up to 7 miles. A glance at the tables shows why:

Take the Eddystone lighthouse (133ft) with its Light 41 metres above the sea. At 6-miles range its vertical sextant angle is only 12 seconds; an error of observation of 3 seconds would put you a mile out of position. Obviously index error must be applied. But it can be invaluable if struggling to round a headland in a fickle wind and foul tide by setting the sextant on its highest point and using it to show whether progress is being made or lost.

The same technique can be used against other yachts while racing.

See also horizontal sextant fixes on pages 59, 60.

Ability to cope with the weather as it comes is a major part of the navigator's problem. The very word covers a host of overlapping factors from visibility to moisture content, wind speed to sea-state, air and sea temperatures, to the passage of depressions with their associated fronts and the effects of ocean currents.

You may enjoy the weather and derive great assistance from the Trade Winds. Or you can be terrified while suffering unimaginable discomfort from it, be weather-bound, look weather-beaten or have trouble getting to weather of a hazard. The very word is all-pervading, dominating every moment of a sailor's life, especially if he is in a small underpowered yacht.

The strength and direction of the wind most concerns those who sail in tall ships, as Cruiser Trewsbury found once he cast off from the sinking Clipper *Blackgauntlet* in her longboat:

Hitherto [in clipper ships] he had dealt with the wind … wrestling to use it and master its power and fury. Now [in an open boat] the real enemy was the seething leaping and appalling water, so close at hand. All that waste of tumult was the enemy … about to pounce.
– from John Masefield's immortal *Bird of Dawning*.

So it is with yachts. A maxi concerns itself mainly with using the wind to best advantage, but the smaller the yacht and the shorter its sail-plan the more it must recognize the sea as the element to respect most.

There are well-attested formulae showing the relationship between wind and sea, but the fine print under them usually warns that they relate to conditions offshore. Local weather, tides and the depth of water can produce seas which are not theoretically possible in the windspeed prevailing. The start

of the 1951 Fastnet was delayed for 6 hours, during which the sou'westerly gale gusted 68 knots at Calshot and all small classes' racing was abandoned, but not before the Dragons had gone out and one was sunk without trace off the Castle. The crew of Gerald Potter's new Laurent Giles-designed *Fandango* (33ft 6in LWL) passed the time visiting a friend's boat on an adjacent mooring in the Roads, the lovely Nicholson-designed *Old Fox*. The rain was so heavy and her deckheads leaked so badly that we wore sou'westers and oilskins as we sat in her saloon and drank the owner's vintage Krug.

When we at last were sent away, the beat down the Solent was under a full ebb tide. Here we suffered not so much from the height of the seas (probably 12ft off Hurst Castle) as the short interval (or period, as it's called) between them. Due to a combination of shallow water and wind-against-tide, the seas were vicious, steep and tumbling in one after the other. The book says that offshore there would have been over 20 seconds between successive wave-tops, each of them 500 yards apart. On this occasion the wave interval was probably not much over 3 seconds and their length 2–3 boatlengths. The bone-shaking slamming was worse than anything I ever experienced in an offshore powerboat race. One of the crew then went to use the heads in the forepeak, a beautiful glazed porcelain bowl with a violet flower pattern and gleaming varnished seat, probably left over from a batch run up for the old Royal Yacht *Victoria & Albert*. At the critical moment the whole bowl disintegrated, leaving only a jagged porcelain stump. Fortunately I was gripping an overhead grabrail at the time, so was left swinging precariously, but still entire, over its razor-sharp remains. The next time I saw a loo like that was on an Aeroflot flight from Moscow to Tbilisi, but I would expect to find them on the Orient Express. Neither the Russian copy of our Comet nor the Wagon-Lit coaches shuttling down to Venice is designed to pull the number of g's we did, probably 7 negative.

The point of the story is that once we were clear of the Needles and beating far to the south of Portland Bill, the tide turned foul and the seas flattened out even though the wind was still over 50 knots. Or so we guessed, having no anemometer in those days.

The bottom affects the wave size and behaviour once the depth of water is under half the length of the waves. Much was written about the part played by the Labadie Bank in the 1979 Fastnet disaster, even though the official enquiry discounted it. The least depth on the bank is 200ft. A wave behaves like a shallow-water one breaking over a sandbank when its length is 25 times the depth of water. On that day in August the waves would have had to be a mile long to fall into that category as they swept over the Bank. In fact they were about 200yds long and 20ft high, rolling majestically in an ESE'ly direction when we surfed across it. Its main significance at that point is that it stands up like an underwater island from surrounding water of 400ft in depth, so the echo-sounder fix crossed with a radio D/F bearing on Round Island 75 miles away is a good start for planning an accurate landfall at the Bishop Rock.

Anyway the yachts which got into trouble were all far to the east of the Labadie Bank in water deeper than 300 feet. But, like the Bermuda Triangle, the myth will persist as long as there is oil in the saloon lamp.

Other dangerous sea states outside their context are to be found in the confluence of tidal streams off a headland. St Catherine's, Barfleur, St Alban's Point and the Lizard can all give the navigator trouble and dump cook's curried stew on to the cabin sole, even though they are not as notorious as Portland Bill or the Alderney Race.

So, when planning a voyage, don't think you have all the weather data you need just by listening to the Shipping Forecast. Use the tide to your advantage and comfort. Crossing from the Solent to the Channel Islands, if the wind is W'ly catch the first of the flood off Nab Tower or the Needles which will give you 6 hours of relatively easy motion (and therefore faster sailing) than you would with wind against tide. If there's an E'ly and it looks like persisting, catch the early Channel ebb.

Scales and other definitions

The most famous yardstick for measuring wind and sea states is the 1805 Beaufort Scale named after the Hydrographer of the Navy in early Victorian days, Rear-Admiral Sir Francis Beaufort (1774–1857), a man of many parts, since he was the first to observe and codify the changing pattern of magnetic variations all over the world.

Notes: Wind speeds are taken at 33ft above sea level.

The approximate wave-heights and periods given above are clear of the land. In shallow water both can be substantially different, as discussed earlier. These are average wave-heights. For the maximum liable to be encountered, add half again. Thus waves in Wind Force 8 should be 18ft from crest to trough, but the rogue wave in the same wind strength could be 25ft.

BEAUFORT SCALE

Force	Wind Speed in kts	Wind Condition	Sea Conditions	Approx Wave ht feet (metres)	Sea State	Period (secs)
0	0–1	**Calm**	Smooth, mirror-like sea.	—		
1	1–3	**Light Air**	Scale-like ripples; no foam crests.	$\frac{1}{4}$	0	
2	4–6	**Light Breeze**	Short wavelets; glassy crests; non-breaking.	$\frac{1}{2}$ (0.2)	1	
3	7–10	**Gentle Breeze**	Large wavelets; glassy crests, some breaking; occasional white foam.	2 (0.6)		
4	11–16	**Moderate Breeze**	Small waves becoming longer; frequent white foam crests.	$3\frac{1}{2}$ (1)	2 / 3	3 / 4
5	17–21	**Fresh Breeze**	Moderate waves with more pronounced long form; many white foam crests; some spray.	6 (1.8)	4	5
6	22–27	**Strong Breeze**	Large waves form; white foam crests everywhere; probably more spray.	$9\frac{1}{2}$ (2.9)	5 / 6	6 / 7
7	28–33	**Near Gale**	Sea heaps up; white foam from breaking waves is blown in streaks with the wind.	$13\frac{1}{2}$ (4)		10 / 11
8	34–40	**Gale**	Moderately high waves with greater length; edges of crests break into spindrift; foam is blown in well-defined streaks with the wind.	18 (5.5)	7	
9	41–47	**Strong Gale**	High waves; crests of waves start to topple and roll over; spray may affect visibility.	23 (7)	8 / 9	15 / 18
10	48–55	**Storm**	Very high waves; overhanging crests; resulting foam is blown in dense white patches with the wind; sea surface takes on a whiter look; the tumbling of the sea becomes heavy and shock-like; visibility affected.	29 (8.8)		20
11	56–63	**Violent Storm**	Exceptionally high waves; sea covered with long white patches of foam blown in direction of wind; all wave crests are blown into froth; visibility affected.	37 (11.4)		23
12	64+	**Hurricane**	Air is filled with spray and foam; sea is completely white with driving spray; visibility seriously affected.	45 (13.5)		25

Sea-states are commonly quoted in N America but are never used in weather bulletins in Britain. Unfortunately they do not equate with wind forces. The following table gives a more precise relationship:

Sea-state	Wave-height	
2	$1\frac{1}{2}$–$3\frac{1}{2}$ft	(0.5–1.0m)
3	$3\frac{1}{2}$–$5\frac{1}{2}$ft	(1.0–2.3m)
4	$5\frac{1}{2}$–$7\frac{1}{2}$ft	(1.6–2.3m)
5	$7\frac{1}{2}$–13ft	(2.3–4m)
6	13–18ft	(4–6m)
7	18–42ft	(6–13m)
8	42–65ft	(13–20m)
9	65–130ft	(20–40m)

Temperature Scales

Converting degrees Fahrenheit to Centigrade
My rule of thumb is to double the Centigrade reading and add 30 to get the Fahrenheit equivalent, but this table may be more accurate:

°F	0	5	10	15	20	25	30	35	40	45	50
°C	−18	−15	−12	−9.4	−6.7	−4	−1	1.7	4.4	7.2	10

°F	55	60	65	70	75	80	85	90	95	100
°C	12.8	15.6	18.3	21	24	26.7	29.4	32.2	35	37.7

The exact ratio is $°F = \frac{9°}{5} C + 32$.

Effective temperature
The wind has a measurable effect on the temperature you feel, as any golfer playing St Andrew's will tell you. The following table gives a fair indication of the Wind Chill Factor. The numbers should be added or subtracted from the temperature noted in a sheltered spot, measured in degrees Fahrenheit.

Wind Speed		Temperature (°F)					
mph	(kts)	+30	+20	+10	0	−10	−20
10	(9)	+16	+2	−9	−22	−31	−45
20	(17)	+3	−9	−24	−40	−52	−68
30	(26)	−2	−18	−33	−49	−63	−78
40	(35)	−4	−22	−36	−54	−69	−87
50	(44)	−7	−24	−38	−56	−70	−88

The Barometer

Barometric scales

Nowadays the barometric pressure reported in the UK is always in millibars (mbs). But it was not always thus. Indeed the USA still talk of 'inches of mercury' and even modern barometers show the pressure both in mbs and inches. Less frequently the pressure may be quoted in millimetres (mm) of mercury. Here is a scale. In case you lose it, 1in of mercury = 34mbs.

Inches	Mbs	Mms
28.05	950	712
28.35	960	719
28.65	970	727
28.05	980	738
29.23	990	743
29.52	1000	749
29.81	1010	757
30.12	1020	764
30.41	1030	772
30.71	1040	779
31.00	1050	787

The centre of a depression or *Low* is commonly about 970mbs, whilst the famous Azores *High* which is supposed to drift northwards in summer to let us stow away foul-weather gear occasionally is often around 1030mbs. But don't be startled to hear 1005 quoted as a *Low*; it may well be if it is paired off with a *High* of 1040 in the same part of the world.

The old mercurial barometer housed in a black tube and secured vertically to a bulkhead on gimbals is now only seen in museums, pubs, the porch of a retired Admiral's house in

Barometer needle   **Marking pointer set by hand**

Barometer

the Meon valley or antique shops.

Nowadays aneroid barometers with a single needle show the pressure on a scale marked off clockwise, generally from around 900 to 1050mbs. Often the inches are shown on a concentric scale with such time-honoured but fatuous bromides as 'Set Fair' around 1040mbs through 'Change' to 'Stormy' at 960mbs. There is a second and shorter pointer which can be used to set manually against the sensitive needle. The idea is that you tap the face of the barometer and the needle overcomes any friction to enable it to show the correct pressure at the time. The other pointer will then show whether the pressure has gone up or down since it was last set.

In a boat it is a good idea to read the barometer every hour at sea and enter the reading in the log, but only reset the pointer at much longer intervals, say every 4 or 6 hours.

Otherwise every passing crew member will reset it each time he reads it and you are not left with a sufficiently clear indication of the pressure behaviour.

To be pedantic, the barometer should be adjusted to read correctly at sea-level (there is a zero screw on most), but unless you are taking one from your boat to go flying, or plan to cruise in either the Dead Sea or Lake Titicaca you can safely assume that you are at sea level and the barometer reading needs no adjustment.

What matters is to be able to record changes of barometric pressure, rather than worry about the absolute accuracy of the reading.

Looking at my log of the 1979 Fastnet I see that the barometer read 990mbs at midnight close SE of Cape Clear, then fell 10mbs in 2½ hours as we were hit by the centre of the notorious Low 'Yankee' whose associated front did all the damage. Official meteorological jargon describes any fall of 6mbs in 3 hours as 'very rapid', so we were clearly on a hiding to nothing, with the barometer falling twice as fast as the gloomiest language the Met Office permit themselves. For the record a 'slow' rise or fall is less than 1mb change in 3 hours; a 'quick' one is 3.5 to 6mbs in the same time, until it goes off the clock as above. At the time, the barometer's behaviour had all the fascination of watching the needle of a submarine's depth-gauge go down out of control.

Rather than make your on-board forecasts based on logged barometer readings, you can have them graphically displayed on a barograph plotting millibars against time. Mostly they have a clockwork-driven drum carrying a week's squared paper with a stylus tracing the pressure all the time. These are interesting but have drawbacks: no one is quite certain how much heavy weather motion they can stand up to, although makers claim they have them damped and resiliently mounted. Certainly they need to be securely installed well

Barograph

away from any other leads or sheets which might snag them. At around £300 they cost about 5 times as much as an analogue barometer.

Weather Forecasting

Some owners never miss a BBC Shipping Forecast while they are on board. By contrast Rod Stevens used not to allow a radio receiver on board for fear of the navigator or skipper taking the weather forecasts seriously and acting too soon by reducing sail on a storm warning, or too late in shaking out the reefs.

In the 1950s the Southsea-Brixham Race was won easily by *Prelude*. She was the only yacht in the fleet without a radio, so received no warning of a severe gale which never developed. All the others either put into Cherbourg or reefed down to a standstill.

There are those who are uneasy if they have not nodded sagely over the synoptic chart, whether received on board by facsimile (weather fax), pinned up at the fuel pontoon in the marina or published alongside the crossword puzzle in the daily paper. Like all such graphic presentations they are no better than the met men ashore who have interpreted all the reports from weather ships, reporting stations and satellite observations. The end result is a synoptic chart showing the centres of Lows and Highs surrounded by isobars, which are contour-lines showing where the barometric pressure is the same (see p. 111). Since the wind flows towards areas of low pressure and away from the Highs it is necessary to understand two facts which follow this unsurprising doctrine:

(1) The greater the change in adjacent areas of barometric pressure the stronger the wind will blow to keep nature's weather systems in balance. So, close isobars mean strong winds. How strong can be reliably measured on a logarithmic scale usually printed on the synoptic chart.

(2) Due to the earth's rotation the winds do not flow directly towards the centre of a Low at sea level. They also lose some of their power due to friction of the earth's surface. They form an anticlockwise pattern around the Low's centre. Imagine it as a horde of Apaches racing in a circle around a beleaguered wagon train carelessly loosing off arrows inwards, but forgetting to allow for the 20 knots forward velocity of their horses – so their arrows don't go straight into the wagons, but obliquely at an angle of about 25° tangential to each contour or isobar. With a High system the winds blow outwards and clockwise to the area of high pressure, again about 25° away from the tangent.

As with the story about the swirl of the bath-water going down the drain, in the Southern Hemisphere it's all the other way round.

When interpreting a synoptic chart there are some simple notations which will help you assess the weather it is likely to presage.

Wind direction and strength are shown as arrows pointing the right way, with feathers sticking out of their weather ends. Each full feather denotes 2 points on the Beaufort Scale. Thus $3\frac{1}{2}$ feathers would show Force 7.

In our waters depressions (Lows) typically move ENE'ly through or to the north of the British Isles at speeds which can be as high as 70 knots, but mostly nearer the speed reported as 'steadily' on shipping forecasts (15–25kts). Sometimes they are held up by a persistent high pressure area and will slow down or even briefly stop. When they are dissipating they are referred to as 'filling', but 'deepening' is bad news – it means the pressure of the low is falling and, with it, the surrounding winds are sure to pipe up.

The master of the *Queen Elizabeth* once told me that he did not bother too much about depressions while on a crossing to the USA, because his ship was through and out the other side in a matter of a couple of hours, with 28 knots traversing an oncoming depression moving at the same speed, making the relative movement of the storm away from the liner nearly a mile a minute. But making a W–E crossing can be tedious. So it was in 1960 sailing *Drumbeat* from Newfoundland to Brixham, we picked up a slow-moving warm front soon after departure and stayed in its clammy claustrophobic grip most of the way across.

Different types of air masses in the vicinity of a Low jostle for position and form distinct boundaries or fronts with predictable weather behaviour either side of them. Light warm air advancing in the south side of a Low runs with a cold mass, rises over it and creates heavy rain. The boundary is a warm front shown on weather charts as rounded nodules or bumps on its leading edge. The warm air behind it has little rain, but the wind direction veers markedly. Not far behind

Warm Front:
advancing warm air rides up and over cold air

Cross-section through
the Warm Front

Warm Air

Warm Air

Cold Air

Cold Air

200 Miles Rain or Snow

Cold Front:
advancing cold air pushes under the warm air

Cross-section through
the Cold Front

Cold Air

Warm Air

Occasional embedded
cumulonimbus

Cold Air

Warm Air

200 Miles Showers
50 Miles Heavy Rain

Occluded Front:
cold air has advanced on warm air and lifted it

Cross-section through
the Occluded Front

Cold Air

Cool Air

Warm Air

Warm Air

Cold Air

Cool Air

Rain

will be the cold front, bringing more rain, but clearing rapidly as it goes through and the wind veers still farther.

The cold front is shown as a line drawn out from the Low with spiky markings. When it overtakes and merges with the warm front, it is said to be occluded, shown by alternate spikes and nodules on the chart.

Source of weather forecasts
Around Britain the BBC's long wave 1500m (200kHz) forecasts are the most easily received. These are transmitted every day on clocktime at 0033, 0555, 1355 and 1850. There are inshore waters forecasts on Radio 3 247m (12.15 kHz) at 0655 and on long wave at 0038. Besides the conventions already mentioned, the shipping forecasts use other definitions which it is as well to know:

A gale is said to be 'imminent' if it is expected within 6 hours of the issuing time of the bulletin (usually 1–2 hours before transmission, but always stated).

If it is expected 'soon' it is within 6–12 hours, whilst 'later' means it is over 12 hours away.

In defining the visibility, it is 'moderate' if 2–5 miles, 'good' beyond that and 'poor' down to $\frac{1}{2}$ mile when it is officially fog.

There are many local forecasts obtainable. Details can be found in the *Shell Pilot to the English Channel* at the end of each section devoted to a port.

There is also an excellent new forecasting service obtainable through the telephone network, known as Weathercall for land forecast and Marinecall for sea areas. You can get all coastal regions, including the other side of the Channel, on 0898–500 432 or specific areas by changing the last three digits. For example, 457 covers Lyme Regis to Selsey across to the Channel Islands and Cherbourg peninsula. A long-term forecast covering up to 6 days ahead is available on 0898–500 430.

Storm Cones are black triangular (or by night red lights) hoisted point downwards for gale force winds due from or expected to move towards the south, which actually means anywhere from 091° through 180° to 269°. The cone point up covers gales from all other quarters of the compass.

Old Salts' Tales

There are many catch-phrases which have survived since oilskins and seaboots were invented. They all have an odds-on chance of being right. For instance:

Red sky at night – sailor's delight
Red sky in the morning – sailor's warning

Then there are:

When the wind shifts against the sun,
Trust it not, for back it will run

When the wind follows the sun,
Fine weather will never be done

Long foretold – long past
Short notice – soon past

The cruel one, especially when it happens is:

First rise after very low
Indicates a stronger blow

We all know how an easterly wind pattern can persist:

If the wind be north-east three days without rain,
Eight days will pass before south again.

Clouds (see pp. 115–17)

It is almost self-evident that high white fluffy soft clouds are friends telling you to expect fine weather with light to moderate breezes. Blacker and more ragged clouds presage hard weather.

High clouds moving in a different direction from lower ones indicate a change of wind direction.

A distant depression is often signalled by converging streaks of high cloud meeting at a point well over the western horizon; it may be 500 miles away at that time, but it could be with you in 12 hours.

From a clear blue sky to one in which day has been turned into night there is a wide variety of patterns aloft, any of which may contribute towards the navigator's understanding of what the weather is about to do. All glider pilots and most aviators brought up in unpressurized aircraft are good shipmates when it comes to recognizing turbulence and squalls under certain clouds. Some will go to extraordinary lengths to chase them when there's not much wind around elsewhere.

High Clouds (over 20,000ft) indicate gentle conditions on deck, but some give early warning of changes to come.

Cirrus (Ci) are delicate white clouds which sometimes form those mares' tales with which old salts pepper their yarns. They tell you that there's a lot of wind up there, but nothing much will happen on deck in your watch.

Cirro-stratus (Cs) occurs when all the cirrus has spread into one transparent cloud covering most of the upper sky. Especially when accompanied by halos it indicates unsettled, deteriorating weather for sure.

Cirro-cumulus (Cc) are banks of small white clouds forming parallel bands across the sky, similar to patterns seen at low tide on some sandy beaches. Changeable weather is on the menu, especially when it moves briskly.

Medium Clouds are those which determine one's comfort when flying in a light aircraft, being between 7,000 and 20,000 feet above sea level.

Alto-cumulus (Ac) are layers of grey or white clouds, similar

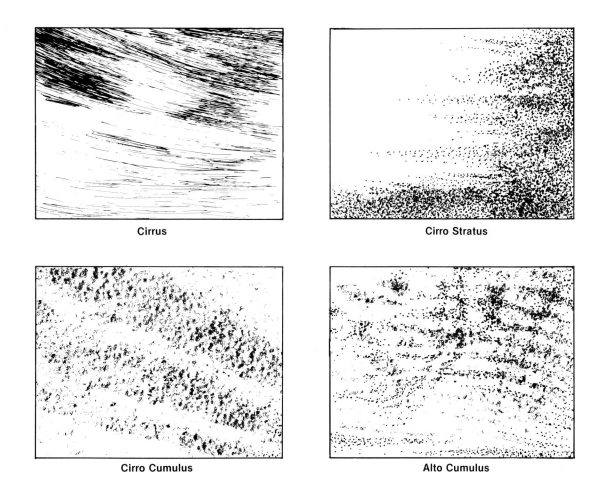

Cirrus

Cirro Stratus

Cirro Cumulus

Alto Cumulus

Alto Stratus

Strato Cumulus

Cumulus of the Doldrums

Cumulus

Stratus

Cumulo Nimbus

Line Squall

to cirro-cumulus, but much lower. Sometimes known as a mackerel sky, it presages rain. If it forms patterns like the battlements of a castle, stand by for thunderstorms.

Alto-stratus (As) is an all-over layer of thin grey cloud through which a watery sun may appear. Rain is a certainty, probably with an approaching front bringing wind with it. When the rain comes, the cloudbase may become very much lower, when it becomes Nimbo-stratus (Ns).

Low Clouds, below 7,000 feet, are the most familiar.

Cumulus (Cu) are the cottonwool clouds with grey bottoms. When they are not too large or reaching for the stars, they mean fair weather. But when they expand to look like giant cauliflowers, watch out for showers.

Cumulo-nimbus (Cb) are instantly recognizable as thunderclouds, high flat-topped and unfriendly. They are to be found in the vicinity of active fronts, invariably with squalls and strong winds.

Stratus (St) are low, grey miserable clouds, often sitting over headlands. They mean drizzle and poor visibility.

Strato-cumulus (Sc) are masses of grey puffy clouds, frequent in winter on those raw days of drizzle or sleet.

But the most welcome, and recognizable, sign in the sky is when the rain-clouds end in a hard line across the western horizon, giving way to blue skies. That's the end of a front.

Local variations

The most common phenomena to upset the direction and speed of the winds all over the world are land and sea breezes. Not only are most winds much stronger away from land, excepting only those generated by a funnelling effect in high-sided estuaries, but their direction and strength will change as the sun climbs into the sky. This is especially true when the underlying wind in the area is light. As the land warms up the sea breeze will fill in on an onshore direction, usually for about a mile, but sometimes as much as 10 miles. At night the reverse is true, with a local land breeze blowing offshore as the land cools off. This can play a vital part in racing, and it's worth recalling when cruising once the log-speed drops below 2 knots.

The 1973 220-mile Seine Bay Race started off Southsea in near calm conditions. It ended 36 hours later with Sir Max Aitken's brand new 52-ft ketch *Perseverance* taking all the prizes by finishing over 2 hours ahead of the next boat.

'At last', the yachting correspondent of one of the nationals commented with unconscious irony, 'Sir Max has got the boat he richly deserves.'

'Rocket ship', declared the designer modestly as he stepped ashore.

What actually happened was that our top Solent tactician, Bobby Lowein, opted to work across towards the Isle of Wight shore in anticipation of a land breeze developing out of Bembridge, since it had been a hot cloudless day. Alone of the fleet we slowly crabbed our way across the fairway into slack water off St Helen's, the others all having to kedge in a foul tide near the Outer Spit buoy. Sure enough, an hour after dark a private reaching breeze sent us tramping on starboard tack, leaving the whole fleet for dead.

Unhappily it was the only major race she ever won, soon revealing most of the nasty habits ever built into a boat. To be competitive we needed to find 10 feet off her IOR rating. But she had her moment, thanks to our punting on the land breeze and ignoring the rhumb-line.

The strength of land and sea breezes are in proportion to the contrast between day and night temperatures along the coast. There is one feature to be borne in mind: if there has already been a steady onshore wind all day as part of the local weather pattern, it may do no more than reduce its strength after nightfall, while the reverse will be found some hours after dawn if the sea breeze makes up in the same direction as the prevailing wind.

The global distribution of pressure and weather systems is well known, from the Doldrums of the equator, through the Trade Winds either side of them to the Horse Latitudes. The British Isles lie in a belt modestly understated as Variable Westerlies, while the matching zone in the Southern Hemisphere is more aptly named as The Roaring Forties. All these have logical effects on ocean currents, the most famous of which is the Gulf Stream, funnelled NNE'ly between Florida and the Bahamas. Its warm core sinuates in a broad clockwise sweep across the North Atlantic before splitting. One arm gives the farmers as far north as Tromsö relatively easy winters and little ice in those northern fjords. It is also responsible for the Soviet Navy's having year-round access to the North Atlantic from the Kola Inlet. The other arm swings southwards past Galway and Kerry, sustains the tropical gardens at Tresco, sends early daffodil crops to Covent Garden, thence past the Iberian Peninsula before turning west near the Cape Verde Islands to pick up a fresh load of Sargassum weed and go round the track again.

The area of benign trade winds is also the breeding-ground of savage hurricanes and cyclones with winds up to 170 knots, moving on (nowadays) well-reported tracks at speeds up to 300 miles per day during their appointed seasons. It is relatively simple and obviously prudent planning to avoid being exposed to these king-size storms.

Each year thousands of yachtsmen in small boats make the Trade Wind crossing from the Canaries to the Carribean during our winter, outside the hurricane season. Most of them confidently look forward to successive days of brilliant sunshine, running wing-and-wing or tacking downwind across a cobalt sea with little to worry about beyond when to deep-six the bananas or whether the cold beer and suntan lotion will last the trip. Weather forecasts are not worth listening to.

In November 1979 I was two-thirds of the way to English Harbour, Antigua, in the Swan 47 *Toscana* when a local storm hit us in the middle of the night. It behaved like a junior hurricane, gusted 50 knots and boxed the compass before leaving us within the hour to reset the sails, steady on 270° and get back into routine: identify the seabirds, pick up the dead flying-fish (delicious filleted and sautéed in butter), call the cook early and recalculate one's bet on the sweep for the noon-to-noon run. Research in the *Admiralty Sailing Directions* turned up an Inter Tropical Convergence Zone (ITCZ) storm, so local as often to go unreported.

Such local freak storms can be found all over the world, many of them of lethal severity. The NW'ly mistral in the Gulf of Lions in winter and spring, the E'ly levanter bringing low cloud over the Rock of Gibraltar, the SE'ly sirocco and NE'ly gregale around Malta, the icy tramontana in the Tyrrhenian and Adriatic Seas, williwaws off Patagonia, not to mention willy-willies off Queensland. Each has the power to hit like a heavyweight, landing the winning punch before his opponent has come out for the bell at the start of the round.

So it was at 1245 two days after Christmas 1977, in the Holland-designed Two-Tonner *Knockout*. We had reason to be pleased with our progress that far in trying to take the Sydney-Hobart trophy back to Britain. We had put 150 miles between us and the overkill of Sydney hospitality on a brilliant sunny day, 30 miles off the coast of New South Wales, with Mount Dromedary abaft the beam. Fixes showed that we had got the current we had come for. At 1110 the NW'ly breeze faltered, so we set the light blooper and $\frac{1}{2}$oz spinnaker, gossamer-light but drawing like a poultice.

I was regaling the afterguard with how I first heard of fabric being like gossamer – in a mail-shot from a chemist in Piccadilly just after my engagement had appeared in *The Times*. Regular supplies of their product were offered in plain envelopes. The sales-pitch ended with: 'Finally, may we wish you every conceivable joy'. At noon the weather forecast was for easterlies 25–30 knots off Gabo Island, 100 miles farther down the track, with a new front the next day bringing W or SW winds 20–30 knots, later going W or NW and moderating.

'That's an odd cloud across the horizon ahead', someone remarked. I had the *Australian Sailing Directions* in the cockpit, open at the picture of a typically white and inviting cloud formation heralding a Southerly Buster. A mile ahead a boat was seen to drop her spinnaker and harden in. Bobby Lowein, the best of many superb ocean-racing skippers I have been lucky enough to navigate for, called immediately for three reefs in the main and the tiny armour-plated No. 6 jib.

As the ripples came at us across the glassy sea, we just got the $\frac{1}{2}$oz down before being hit by a 40-knot southerly, right on the nose, building to a steady Force 10 in as many minutes.

The 1979 Fastnet should be in the *Guinness Book of Records* as the sporting event which claimed the greatest number of participants' lives – fifteen. Of the 302 boats which set out, 218 were officially deemed to have 'retired', a euphemism which included 5 sunk and 18 abandoned mostly with crippling damage. The forecasters' gale warnings, based on synoptic charts available to them, were too little and too late, nor were they sufficiently ominous. The official enquiry reached a few surprisingly complacent conclusions:

> In the Western Approaches to the British Isles gales which arrive with little warning are a feature of our weather which those who sail must expect to encounter from time to time.
>
> We can find insufficient evidence to lead us to recommend any alteration in the size limits for entrants.

Others did, noting that all the fatalities and all but one of the boats abandoned were in the three smallest Classes – under 30ft rating at the time, or One-Ton size and smaller. The lesson of the Sydney–Hobart Race only eighteen months previously had not been taken in. This time there were no handy ports of refuge to run for.

Here's how I saw it, as recorded in my deck-log of the same *Toscana*, whose strong crew included John Rousmaniere, author of the best book about the disaster (*Fastnet–Storm 10*). Soon after midnight on my birthday, 13 August, we rounded Land's End and headed for the Fastnet Rock 150 miles away to the NW. A reaching SW breeze Force 4/5 died at breakfast-time, soon after the morning BBC Shipping Forecast, which spoke of SW 4–6. By noon the wind had backed to SSE 5–6, then veered to SW in 10 minutes, blowing out the $\frac{3}{4}$oz chute.

At 1355 there was mention of a Low 300 miles to the west, but our area forecast remained SW 4–5, increasing 6–7 and going to the west. As we listened we were already sailing in a W × S wind Force 6, which then died to light southerlies.

At 1750 we got our first gale warning associated with Low 'Yankee', now said to be 250 miles west of the Fastnet. Our area (Lundy/Fastnet) was booked for S'ly Force 4, locally 6, increasing to gale Force 8 before going NW. At dusk the wind was still S'ly, but gusting over 40 knots, as we reeled off 9 knots along the rhumb-line with a single-reefed main.

By midnight the barometer had fallen 10mbs in $2\frac{1}{2}$ hours to 980mbs and we had a whole SSW'ly gale on our hands. Our sail plan now consisted of the smallest jib on the inner headstay, with all three reefs pulled down on the main. Sure enough, the 0015 Shipping Forecast told us what we already knew, except that Force 10 was mentioned for the first time. But we were comforted by the fact that the nearest reporting station (Valencia) only had S × E Force 6, although its barometer was 986mbs and 'falling rapidly'.

The abrupt wind-shift which did all the damage hit us about 10 miles ESE of the Rock. Five hours after rounding it the barometer had risen 12mbs to 994mbs.

Even if we had a radio weather-fax receiver we should have been none the wiser, for the official synoptic chart for midnight (see p. 111) did not carry any symbols for winds above Force 7, although the passage of the cold front which triggered off the cataclysmic wind veer is plain to see. When redrawn after the event, the wind velocities were remeasured from the isobars and nearly justified the velocities the fleet had to survive. Later Alan Watts produced an interesting theory that there had been undetected 'ripples' along the isobars, which brought them very much closer to each other in places than the faired off lines on the synoptic chart indicated. Obviously, wherever that happened there would be gusts of great severity, which, he argued, would account for boats near each other reporting widely differing wind speeds.

I buy that. But the real lesson of both these big storms is that on-board observation of the behaviour of the barometer and reading the cloud formations should have been enough to warn us. That's all very well if you're still in harbour or in coastal waters, but once offshore with nowhere to hide perhaps it's as well to imagine you are sailing with Rod Stevens and take the weather as it comes. No yacht can sail fast enough to clear the front of an advancing storm. Besides noting the behaviour of your own barometer, be on the alert whenever land reporting stations report widely differing barometer readings on the same Shipping Forecast.

Ever since that Fastnet I suspect the lads at the Met Office have hedged their bets with such qualifying asides as: 'Winds sou'west 4 to 5, perhaps locally 7 or 8 at times'. That suffix would justify a gale warning being issued for the area, which played havoc with the jetfoil sailings on the Dover–Ostend route when they first started operating and were told not to sail if there was a gale warning in force. Bracknell-watchers claim to be able to identify the Duty Forecaster by the degree of wariness built into his script.

I have not done a proper analysis, but I rely on Shipping Forecasts' being right about 60% of the time. They claim 80% accuracy for land forecasts. The rest of the time they can lead people to hold on to a course far from the rhumb-line in anticipation of a wind-shift or encourage them to persist with the wrong sail-plan long after it should have been changed.

Mostly, however, the forecasts tell you about the weather you've already got. And they do not have the data needed to give any warning about the seas likely to be encountered. So the combination of an angry sea from the WNW clashing with 20ft swells from the SSW, which really killed most of the Fastnet fleet, could not possibly have been hinted at in any of the bulletins.

Currents

Of all the natural phenomena associated with the weather, the most predictable in their behaviour, next to the times of sunrise and sunset, are the currents, whether wind-generated or tidal. The latter may be held up by persistent contrary winds and their heights vary in bottleneck harbours, but, as a rule, they come and go as stated in the tables and tidal atlases.

The direction of the various ocean currents may be relied on, although strengths may vary in proportion to surface winds' persisting for any length of time. The most famous of these is the Gulf Stream, especially as it affects yachts cruising or racing off the eastern seaboard of the United States with the violent local electric storms which prowl along its edges. The Newport–Bermuda Race is rarely won or lost without the Stream's playing a part. It has a hot core of water about 10 miles wide carrying stream current water at its maximum of about 4 knots. Its presence is marked by a sudden jump in seawater temperature at its so-called West Wall (the side facing the USA). This can be as much as 8–10° in a few hours, but the corresponding drop on the Bermuda side of the core is not so marked and probably not more than 5° at the most.

The catch is that the core rarely flows steadily in a WSW–ENE'ly direction until it is well past Bermuda, but meanders as much as 70° off course for a distance of 30 miles or more, before swinging back to rejoin the grain of the Stream. Sailing down from Newport, one's trick is to hit off the SE'ly meander and ride it for all it's worth, making 11–12 knots over the ground. If you guess wrong you will have to plug a foul current for many hours. Sometimes the Stream water breaks away and forms circular eddies as much as 40 miles in diameter. Warm eddies rotate clockwise, so to hitch a ride on them you must hit one off nearly tangential to its eastern perimeter. Cold eddies are anticlockwise, so must be approached from their western side. This feature gave the race some unlikely winners and the soubriquet among the losers of being the 'Gulf Stream Crapshoot'.

Recently the element of luck has been reduced by the Ocean Services Unit of the National Oceanic and Atmospheric Administration (NOAA) in Washington using its computers to produce tidal charts of the Stream based on data from satellite surveillance. The lat-long of the points along the West Wall and the centres of the identifiable eddies are broadcast on radio twice a day. With all that information on your plot, all you need do is navigate the boat to the point where it starts to be boosted along by favourable currents. Given Loran-C in good form, that is child's play.

As always, there are snags. The whole boiling issue moves in a generally ENE'ly direction at speeds which cannot be predicted with certainty. So if the satellite has an off-day or has trouble delivering the raw data through total cloud cover, your plot may be 2–3 days out of date, thus leaving you guessing.

In the 1984 Race there was a hefty SE'ly meander to be found just west of the rhumb-line. Most of the fleet hit it off, only to be greeted with 30–35kt SE'ly winds over the deck all the way to the finishing line. That was a classic wind-against-tide situation, beating all the way down what is traditionally a brisk reaching course. It was a bit like opting to go through the Portland Race to get a fair tide. When the boat stopped slamming like a destroyer, it meant you'd left the strongest part of the current and it was time to tack back for more.

By contrast, the 1986 Race laid on a barely discernible meander, but a huge cold eddy to the south of it. It was a reaching and running race of light airs. Armed with a private long-range met forecast of uncanny accuracy we caught all the wind-shifts very early, hit off the western side of the cold eddy and finished fourth in the hottest IOR Class in an 8-year-old boat.

Although many cruising yachtsmen read about the Bermuda Race, their main interest lies in knowing where to put all the Gulf Stream data in perspective in planning a Transatlantic passage. It may be summed up as follows:

(a) Its mean velocity is at its greatest between the Florida Keys and a point about 200 miles NNE of Bermuda, having swept close past the notorious Cape Hatteras. In that area will be found not only severe local storms and heavy seas, but always a strong current in a broadly NNE'ly direction, slowly turning eastwards.

(b) If on a west-to-east Transatlantic passage it is always worth putting up with local discomfort for the bonus of its current. At least the seas in it are warm and there is a lot of sunshine between squalls. On an east-west crossing keep well clear, either using the Great Circle route far to the north, or the balmier Trade Wind crossing about 1,000 miles north of the equator. Many people make the mistake of an intermediate course from the Azores to the west. That usually means the worst of both worlds.

(c) If you have to cross the Stream, treat it just like any other tidal current by laying off the amount you expect to be pushed laterally and adjusting course accordingly.

(d) Be on the conservative side with the sail area carried through the Stream at night, unless you have a strong and alert crew.

Summary of on-board weather forecasting

Assuming a North Atlantic depression moving in a generally easterly direction, a tabulated check-list of the points to look for and what they mean is overleaf

Humidity Professional forecasters set great store by observing changes in the atmosphere's relative humidity, but the instruments involved are not suitable for carrying in a yacht, so this aspect has been ignored.

Factor	Warm Front	Cold Front	Aftermath
Wind	Veers to SW and increases	Veers from SW to W or NW. Squalls, then decreases	Steady direction, moderating slowly
Barometer	Rapid fall ahead of the front	A sudden rise with the passage of the front	Gradually steadies
Air temperature	Warmer	Suddenly cooler	Steady
Visibility	Getting worse	Marked improvement behind the front	Much better
Sky and clouds	Clouding over from Cirrus to Nimbo-stratus	Strato-cumulus and Cu-nim in the front	Cumulus or blue sky
Rain	Steady, turning to drizzle on arrival of the front	Heavy rain	Occasional showers

First thoughts

Assuming you are not bent on qualifying for membership of the LYS (see back cover), the navigator has a formidable check-list to complete before setting sail for more than a day's picnic.

(1) *Destination* Decide on sensible limits for your cruise, with the equivalent of diversionary airfields firmly identified. If any one in the crew has to be back in his office by a certain time, be sure there is no misunderstanding on that score. If he elects to come as far as Camaret with you, he'd better have his own plans for getting home, rather than rely on the boat to divert to Roscoff for him to catch a ferry. In any event, keep 48 hours in hand to allow for adverse weather on the return journey.

(2) *Speed of advance (SOA)* While the carefree, one-day-at-a-time philosophy underlines the fact that you are cruising and not racing, it is as well to have a general understanding with the crew whether you are setting out on a voyage with a planned SOA of 4, 5½ or 7 knots. Some people think flopping around in mid-Channel with a stalled anemometer is fun. Actually it is moderately dangerous, and the boat's motion can be tiresome. So have a clear policy about when the iron spinnaker is going to be pressed into service. Is it to be if the speed falls below 3 knots for, say, half an hour?

(3) *Route planning* Do your preliminary planning on a small-scale chart covering the farthest extent of your cruise. For the English Channel Imray produce two excellent passage charts (C10 and 12) covering the whole area at 1:310,000 scale (4nm to the inch). When you have a firm plan, buy the publications and large-scale charts you really need. At £6.90 each (and no doubt rising) you should shop carefully. The other day I drew up a list of the absolute minimum inventory of charts and publications needed to get a friend's yacht from the Canaries to Dubrovnik, via the Balearics and Crete. The bill came to £78.

(4) *Advice from the RYA* If you plan to go anywhere between the Bay of Biscay and West Germany, it is worth laying out £2.50 to get the Royal Yachting Association's publication *Going Foreign*, Vol 1 (C1/87). It is available, along with other volumes covering different parts of the world, from the RYA, Victoria Way, Woking, Surrey GU21 1EQ (tel. 04862–5022)

Nearer the time

(1) Check that the crews all have passports. Non-EEC citizens need a current visa for France. Some of them also need visas for Spain. Passports may never be called for unless you want to visit a casino, use a Eurocheque card or return to UK independently.

(2) Advise crews about stowage limitations and what to bring in gear, cash or kind to make it a harmonious cruise. It is not a bad idea to state a per diem mess bill to cover all the expenses you don't expect to meet yourself. Let them know whether they should bring their own bedding and/or safety harnesses. Say when duty free stores might be available. Have a note of their next-of-kin addresses and telephone numbers.

(3) Be sure the ship's papers are in order. If you don't have the official Registration document between hardback covers, you can get on the Small Ships Register through the RYA for a tenner.

(4) Tell crews when to join and precisely where, giving

your marina berth number where available.

(5) Take a British ensign, the national flag(s) of countries to be visited for the starboard yardarm and a 'Q' flag to be shown until cleared by Customs and immigration (police) on arrival. In practice, even at large ports of entry like Cherbourg, let alone small ones like St Vaast, you may have difficulty in finding any one to pay the slightest attention to your arrival. However, you can count on the man collecting harbour dues to show up, and possibly the agent for duty free stores.

(6) Check over all nav-aids, including the charts and electronics, especially the navigation lights. Have the ship's batteries at the top of a charge. Secrete your own private torch, pencil, matches and small batteries.

Last thing

(1) Get a weather forecast from any source you think worth contacting. Try the new Marinecall service on 0898–500 450 for a marine forecast up to five days ahead.

(2) Decide upon and announce the time of sailing, so that you don't have to go ashore and press-gang the other watch.

(3) Clear UK Customs by filling in Part 1 of Form C1528 and deliver it, if not directly to a Customs officer, to one of their mail-boxes, which all marinas have. Keep the rest of the form for completion on return. Failure to do so can have unattractive and far-reaching consequences.

(4) Make sure the right sails are bent on. Decide what to do about the dinghy.

(5) Land all disposable waste.

(6) Top up consumables as required: water, fuel, ice.

(7) Check over emergency drills with the crew: man overboard, fire and collision. Here it might be worth a gentle reminder about the Rule of the Road (International Regulations for Preventing Collisions at Sea), since few yachtsmen know them as well as they should. What lights are shown by a tug with a long tow over 200 metres? Answer: three white vertical lights in place of her masthead light. What fog signal should a sailing yacht make? Answer: one long and two short blasts at intervals of not less than two minutes.

(8) Show where the following are stowed:
Safety harnesses, lifejackets and the liferaft
Torches
Flares
Radar reflector
Foghorn and spare aerosol.

(9) Set the watches. Announce mealtimes and rules about drinking (if any).

of one nautical mile. It is the standard scale for all measurements of distances at sea.

lead-line: a traditional line with 3 kg lead for hand sounding.

leeway: the amount a yacht makes sideways due to the inadequacy of its keel or underwater profile.

LHA: Local Hour Angle, measured E or W in degrees and seconds of arc from the observer's meridian.

LL: the lower limb (edge or rim) of the sun or the moon.

longitude: the E-W scale marked off on parallels of latitude. On a Mercator chart each degree decreases in size as the latitude approaches the poles. Also marked off in 60 seconds of arc for each degree.

Loran-C: the American hyperbolic aid to yacht navigation corresponding to Decca with longer range and different coverage, but comparable accuracy.

lubber's line: the fore-and-aft line in the steering-compass assembly from which the course can be read off.

ma: milli-ampere, a measurement of very small amounts of electrical current.

'mark': the US equivalent of 'cut'.

maxi: a racing yacht of or near 83ft LOA. The generic term for all but the very biggest yachts of over 35m length (megayachts).

mbs: millibars, the unit of barometric measurement.

meander: how the hot, fast core of the Gulf Stream strays off its grain before rejoining it.

Mer-Alt: the meridian-altitude of any heavenly body at its highest.

Mercator: the ancient navigator who introduced charts with all the longitude lines running N and S at right angles to the parallels of latitude.

meridian: a line of longitude.

Mer-Pass: the time of meridian-altitude.

monocular: an optical instrument with a single eyepiece.

Nautical Almanac: a publication giving all the ephemeral data (those which constantly change) for celestial navigation, times of rising and setting. Identical publications under the same name on both sides of the Atlantic.

Navtex: a print-out of weather and navigation messages transmitted by radio and received on board like a telex.

Neaps: the tides having the lowest range, or difference between HW and LW.

NOAA: the National Oceanographic and Atmospheric Administration in Washington, DC, which monitors weather, tides, ocean currents and the environment at sea.

Notices to Mariners (N to Ms): weekly publications put out by the Hydrographer of the Navy carrying all corrections to Admiralty charts and publications.

null: the lowest audible point, sometimes silent altogether, when swinging across a radio bearing for D/F readings.

observed position (Obs Pos): fix using celestial observations only.

parallel ruler: rulers for chartwork which can transfer a course or line of bearing laterally from one part of the chart to another.

pelorus: a stand on which the steering compass is mounted.

period: (1) the interval in seconds between the passing of two successive wave-tops. (2) the time taken for a rhythmic light to complete one complete sequence of its stated characteristics; e.g. Fl(3)W10s means a period of 10 seconds during which there are 3 flashes followed by an eclipse, all adding up to 10 seconds.

perpendicularity: the error in a sextant when the index mirror does not lie in the same plane as the arc showing degrees and minutes of altitude.

polar boat speed: a diagram constructed from theoretical data showing a boat's potential speed at various points of sailing in different winds.

position line: the endless line drawn at right angles to the azimuth of a celestial body used in laying-off the distance equivalent to the intercept. The observer's position lies somewhere on that line.

PPI: Plan Position Indicator. Radar display on cathode ray tube usually with own position in its centre.

protractor: an instrument used for laying off or measuring angles, courses or bearings on a chart.

quadrantal error: the error in radio D/F induced by the materials or method of construction of any yacht.

Racon: a radar beacon on shore which paints its bearing on the PPI of the transmitting yacht's radar. Its effective range is 10 miles.

radar: a transmitted radio impulse which measures range and bearing of any object within its range and usually paints them on to a cathode ray tube, often referred to as a PPI (Plan Position Indicator).

radar interceptor: a receiver intended to warn one that another